The first time . . .

Only a sudden, unexplained flash of rage when Elizabeth was cool to him . . .

The second time . . .

It wasn't so strange, surely, that he was willing to kill the man who had ordered his death . . .

The third time—

when he came out of a blackout to find himself in restraint, facing a shocked girl in a torn dress—made it certain that Kane had fallen victim to

THE PSYCHOPATH PLAGUE

THE PSYCHOPATH PLAGUE

Steven G. Spruill

A DELL BOOK

To John Vetne

Published by
DELL PUBLISHING CO., INC.
1 Dag Hammarskjold Plaza
New York, N.Y. 10017

For information contact Doubleday & Company, Inc.,
245 Park Avenue,
New York, N.Y. 10017.

Dell ® TM 681510, Dell Publishing Co., Inc.

ISBN: 0-440-17230-6

Reprinted by arrangement with
Doubleday & Company, Inc.

Printed in the United States of America
First Dell printing—May 1979

Chapter One

Elias Kane pushed back from the GalTac table and watched the Atlantic cascade off the casino dome while Spencer Hogate waited. Despite the cool, sweat beaded Kane's forehead.

"It's your move," Hogate said.

Polite disapproval rippled through the circle of spectators. Only one watcher—Hogate's massive servant—remained still as he had from the start of the game, pumpkin-colored arms folded, eyes glassy as obsidian. Kane ignored Hogate's gaffe and felt satisfaction. *So Hogate wanted to hurry him. Could it be the man had made a strategic error on the board?* Kane stole a glance at the industrialist; noted the jaw clenched beneath its sheath of fat.

Resisting the impulse to turn back at once to the glittering model of the galactic lens, Kane stretched his shoulders and peered through the dome. The floor stayed perfectly still beneath his boots as the hydraulics bedded in the ocean floor a hundred and fifty meters below continued to thrust the casino upward into daylight. A lone amberjack caught atop the dome flapped soundlessly high above the red carpet and felt tables until it slid down the curvature and plunged into the ocean. Fresh-water jets fountained around the perimeter of the casino and rinsed down the sides of the dome, revealing gray sky and brittle clouds scudding toward the Delaware shore line about two kilometers away. Sparking against the overcast, the morning's first fleet of hoptercabs ferried Earth's bored elite to their amusements. Among such people Kane considered himself an outsider, and yet he wondered now if his passion for this moment, for the chance of doubling or losing everything he had, was really so different from the addictions he had glimpsed in the jaded eyes of others in this place. The thought began to gnaw at his concentration, and he pushed it away. *If he had an addiction, it must surely be the masochistic savagery with which he attacked his own pleasures.*

Kane returned his gaze to the GalTac lens and saw Hogate's mistake at once. The swarm of blue points marking his enemy's holdings in the third quadrant was marred by a thin irregular cylinder of weakness. The last move, in which Hogate had shifted force to counteract a feint toward his mineral star systems, had opened the tunnel; Kane's attack force of three battleships still cloaked in paradoxical space could thrust through it to his opponent's home system in four—no three—moves. Few players would have detected the weakness so soon; Kane took it in with a sweep of his eyes. He pretended to study another section of the lens for a time, then permitted himself a smile. Reaching down to a row of lights lit half along its length, he brushed his finger across the remainder, lighting them all. Another murmur circled the watchers. Hogate seemed more relaxed now—convinced that Kane had not seen his vulnerability. He stared at the row of lights on the bet board and moistened plump lips with the red tongue of a slune addict.

"I will accept your escalation," he said, "but you must grant me a consideration." Kane raised an eyebrow and the other man pressed on. "My funds are temporarily bound up—I have already extended to my limit. However, I am prepared to offer you a quite unique commodity, equal at least in value to your one hundred thousand credits." Hogate paused for effect, sniffed when Kane remained Sphinx-like. "If you win," he continued, "I will deed you my manservant."

Kane could not conceal his surprise. He looked at the orange-skinned giant who had stood unmoving behind Hogate throughout the play. The alien met his gaze and Kane sensed an appeal in the dark eyes beneath their hairless brows. He had noticed earlier the scars along the alien's forearms and wondered how an ox-broad creature who stood well above his own two meters could permit the nervag treatment now eschewed by most owners.

"I would guarantee his monthly allowance of one thousand credits, of course, for as long as both you and he live. As you can see, he is very strong and capable of hard work. He is clever, too, and requires only occasional discipline . . ."

Kane cut him off with a hand motion. "I accept."

Hogate smiled knowingly and nodded. "Good." He inclined his head toward the board. Kane drew a breath, then punched a sequence into his control computer. Yellow lights winked suddenly among the blue; the small cylinder in Hogate's defenses became a gaping hole as the attack and defense boards clicked rapidly back and forth. Jeweled teeth clattered down through the shifting slots of the odds table beneath the galactic lens, and when they lapsed finally into silence, a dozen key planets had fallen to Kane's battleships and the heart of Hogate's empire lay open to a final thrust.

The fat man chewed his lip; his hands fluttered helplessly over the keys of his own board as Kane turned to the alien, ignoring the muted admiration of the gallery.

"What is your name?"

"Pendrake . . . master." The voice was deep and resonant, but gentle.

"I'm not your master," Kane said, testing. "The game is not over."

"In two moves," the alien said.

Hogate shot him a poisonous look. "Until I blank this board, you're mine, you worthless cud. Hold your tongue or I'll . . ."

Kane leaned over and touched Hogate on the shoulder—a friendly gesture which hid the firm pressure on the carotid. "It seems your man Pendrake is cleverer than you thought. His analysis of your situation is correct."

Hogate stiffened and sweat popped out on his neck, but he did not flinch away. "He's no man; he's a cr-creature," he grated.

"Nevertheless, I insist on receiving him in undamaged condition. Otherwise I shall have to summon the adjudicator."

"No, no," Hogate snapped. "With your permission, I'd like to continue the game."

"As you like." Kane dropped his hand, and Hogate returned to the board, ignoring the surprised whispers of the crowd. To persist at this point marked him as a fool at worst or merely stubborn at best. Finally he programed his move—a clumsy counterstroke which permitted Kane to finish him in one play. The board winked yellow and signaled transfer of 100,000 credits and title to Pendrake from Hogate's to Kane's account. The fat man thrust out a silver key and Kane accepted it perfunctorily.

"The creature is yours," Hogate murmured. "I shall honor my bargain as long as you both live." He smiled but his voice was cold.

"Of course," Kane said, feeling mild surprise that the man should feel it necessary to repeat his guarantee. Hogate turned and strode through the group of spectators, which had begun to disperse. Kane closed his eyes and inhaled deeply, savoring the surge of elation. He had risked everything and he had won. The self-doubts had vanished—*only the trapped wolf need bite his own flesh*. When he opened his eyes again, the colors of the vast room seemed supernaturally vivid, the shapes etched in a focus that was almost painfully sharp. Kane smiled and motioned to Pendrake.

"Care for a drink?"

"Master?" The alien appeared shocked. "You are aware, I am sure, that servants may not drink with their masters."

Kane pursed his lips and appeared to consider. "It *would* be a social blunder. I guess I don't have any choice." He reached up and unlocked the brass collar around Pendrake's neck with the key Hogate had given him. The alien stood very still, his eyes fixed, while Kane looked around for a flash unit. He found one by some lounge chairs, dropped the collar in and waited for the pop of molecular disintegration.

"I cannot repay you."

"True. But you can buy me a double shot of twelve-year-old Levian whiskey."

Pendrake bowed.

"I find the top of your head uninspiring," Kane said.

The alien grinned, revealing a set of ivory teeth which joined in an even line unmarred by canines. The effect was a startling contrast from the previous wooden expression. He strode to the drop shaft, leaving Kane to hurry in his wake.

"The Neptune room is on the bottom level," Pendrake said after they had entered the transparent tube and begun to descend. "Master Hogate spent much time there." The alien ran his hand through the thick white hair, which was drawn into a bun behind his ears, and Kane noticed for the first time that each hand possessed only three fingers. He studied Pendrake's face, recalling the page on Cephantine aborigines published in the Spring, 2089, *Journal of Xenobiology*. Cephan, according to the descriptions of those few natives yet to come in contact with humans, was a heavy-gravity Earth-type planet well outside the eight parsec radius beyond which no Earth ship had yet penetrated. The few Cephantines seen by humans had all been slaves accompanying unknown races from the galactic center. Such races appeared infrequently on the borders of the fledgling Terran empire, stopping occasionally to replenish supplies or to note with mild curiosity this latest emerging species, Homo sapiens. Then they would depart again, and sketchy accounts and descriptions would filter back from the pioneer colonies and outposts. Hogate, an interplanetary steel magnate, had evidently procured Pendrake from such an outpost. Perhaps, Kane speculated, the alien had been left by his masters in payment for some necessary raw material supplied by one of Hogate's colony companies.

Pendrake stood without moving as the drop shaft descended, and Kane wondered if the alien was aware of his scrutiny. If so, no trace of self-consciousness marred the serenity of his face; the long space between his upper lip and the delicate, sculpted nostrils was smooth and vaguely simian. The absence of any facial hair gave the face a chiseled look. Kane noticed the edge of a nictitating membrane at the corners of the eyes, a detail not mentioned in the xenobiology report.

The drop shaft hit bottom and they stepped out into a humid but cool sunken garden. On either side of the walk leading away from the shaft were two squat trees unlike any he'd ever seen. The smooth trunks thickened just below the first branches, forming a ball out of which slender stalks laden with maroon blossoms and yellow globes of fruit sprouted in all directions. A spicy-sweet aroma hit his nostrils and he stopped to gaze at the trees. Pendrake paused beside him.

"They are musal trees, Mas—Elias, imported by the Chirpone traders. I believe the fruit is their main dietary staple."

"Don't they need light?"

"They subsist entirely on soil elements and water.

You will note the absence of green leaves or other photosynthetic apparatus."

Kane filled his lungs with the exotic scent, then moved up steps and past a gurgling fountain on the perimeter of the garden. The casino was really a flattened sphere made up of matched domes, the joining of which was presently level with the sea. Altogether, there were ten vast floors, the bottom five always remaining beneath the ocean's surface. The Neptune room offered four crescent-shaped mahogany bars, centered at the points of the compass, which curved gracefully toward each other then back to the perimeter, leaving the space in the middle for the garden. At midday the bars were only partly filled with elegant gentlemen dressed in the popular glossy one-piece skin suits and beautiful women in their mood kilts or leggings and semitransparent halters. Kane's eyes swept the room, noting the subtle similarity of the faces—variations on a few basic themes currently in vogue at the plastic parlors. He fingered his nose where it had been broken during the Tau Ceti affair and remembered with a smile the way the casino plastician had appraised him as he'd strolled past the parlor. *Change the sandy hair to silver-blond and let it cover part of that high forehead,* the man had probably thought. *Straighten the nose, fill out the cheekbones and pad the skin suit to flesh out the body leanness. Oh yes, and some blue contacts to warm up the slate-gray eyes.* Kane shrugged. Beauty was beauty, though he could respect a man like Hogate, who was unconcerned with externals.

He and Pendrake took seats at the nearest bar in a position close to the garden. A red-coated bartender moved over quickly.

"A double Levian green-label for my friend," Pendrake said.

The bartender peered at him. "Say, aren't you Mr. Hogate's . . ."

Kane coughed; the bartender glanced at him, caught the finger he was holding up to his throat. He looked back at Pendrake's neck where the brass collar had been and said, "What'll it be for you?"

"I believe you humans have a cold beverage made from the withered internodes of the Theaceae family. . . ."

A frown began on the bartender's face.

"He'd like iced tea," Kane said.

The bartender repeated their order and moved off, shaking his head.

"I think we'll get along," Kane said.

"You are kind, Elias—an increasing rarity among your species."

Something in the alien's tone alerted Kane. Had he missed something during his year in the desert? "Maybe you haven't given us a chance. Have you known many people besides Hogate?"

Pendrake looked away. "Only a few. My tutor, hired by Mr. Hogate, and the others on his staff."

The bartender returned with their drinks; Pendrake withdrew a five-credit note from a fold in his loose tunic and handed it to the man, who took the corner of the bill, carefully avoiding contact with Pendrake's fingers. Kane noticed that the whiskey was served in a glass, while the tea came in a disposable plastic tumbler. What was wrong with these people, he wondered?

"To your health," Pendrake said, lifting his glass.

"To your health." Kane downed his drink in three

quick gulps, which brought tears stinging to his eyes. Pendrake smiled.

"May I ask how long you have been a wealthy man, Elias?"

Kane looked down at his fashionable silver one-piece, tailored the day before, and at the pliant Saurian boots. Was it so obvious? He frowned. "Two weeks ago I was rounding out a sabbatical in my Arizona shanty when a letter was delivered along with the quarterly batch of journals and books. The letter was from a lawyer and it said that my great-aunt had been separated from her hoard of money in the only way possible. I was the sole inheritor. Today I doubled the money, but until two weeks ago I ate out of redipaks and brewed terrible beer behind the shack to pay for my books."

"You are a student of some discipline, then?"

"I've played a few universities in the past twelve years, but I can't seem to stay in any one field long enough to collect a degree. I have a disease practically extinct in academia—I'm interested in everything." *When I'm interested in anything,* he added to himself.

Pendrake nodded his sympathy. "I have noticed the human mania for specialization. . . ."

There was a stir at the bar; Pendrake and Kane swiveled with the others to watch a retinue of short fat creatures reminiscent of penguins waddle out of the drop shaft accompanied by six reedy-limbed aliens armed with blasters. With the party was a pale woman with striking black hair. Kane recognized her from a pictoral in *WorldNews* a year ago—she was Elizabeth Tyson, noted impresario.

"Chirpones," he murmured. "Who are those skinny characters, though?"

"I believe they are from the planet Krythos, Elias. The Chirpones like to use them as hired bodyguards."

"Damned gooks," a man sitting two stools away from them said in a clear voice. Kane turned and saw that he was looking not at the Chirpones or Krythians but at Pendrake. The man waited a moment and then walked over and positioned himself in front of the big alien. "Oughta go back where they came from."

Kane leaned forward but Pendrake put a hand on his arm. "Pay no attention. It is the plague."

"The plague?"

"The psychopath plague. He is not responsible, Elias."

The man reached out and slapped Pendrake across the face.

Heads swiveled and conversation at the bar died. Kane felt the blood rush to his face, but Pendrake's hand remained firmly on his arm. Marks from the man's fingers made a bright patch on the alien's cheek.

"Not responsible, am I?" the man snarled. "No gook is going to patronize me." The man's motions and speech were steady, Kane saw; not those of a drunk. He was middle-aged, handsome in the plastic-parlor way, but going to fat around the sash on his stylish jump suit.

"Please calm yourself," Pendrake said, gazing at the man as though nothing had happened. There was a stir farther down the bar and a woman hurried forward, slipping herself between the man and Pendrake. Her lips were compressed and bloodless; her hands trembled.

"Stay out of it," the man said. "This *creature* insulted me and I demand satisfaction."

"But since I am merely a creature," Pendrake pointed out, "I cannot give you satisfaction, man to man."

The man hesitated and something seemed to go out of him. "Then I demand an apology."

At that moment the bartender, who had been standing as if frozen, leaned forward. "Why don't we all forget it," he said. "Hards and whiffs on the house." His offer was greeted with a buzz of approval from the other patrons and the scene seemed suddenly to lose its focus as glasses and inhalers clinked and people turned to call in their selections. The man continued to stare at Pendrake for a moment, then yielded to the woman's insistent pressure on his arm and moved off, grumbling.

"You could have rearranged his plasm," Kane murmured. "You're no man's slave, and even if you had been . . ."

"The bartender came forward at an opportune moment."

Kane watched the alien swirl his tea and decided to drop the point. "You said something just before—something about a psychopath plague."

Pendrake studied him. "You *have* been out of touch, Elias. I was referring to the fact that violent crimes, as well as other criminal activities, have been increasing dramatically for the past ten months. The synpapes have only recently discovered the phenomenon—apparently the police have been suppressing the information, but it has reached undeniable proportions."

The bartender set another iced tea and whiskey in front of them and moved down the bar. Kane picked up the amber liquid and studied its core of captured light.

"But why psychopaths? There's no necessary relationship between psychopathy and crime."

"Why should a physically inferior man, who is a stranger to me, try to provoke combat with a creature of my obvious physical strength?"

"Prejudice . . ."

"Pardon me, Elias, but I do not think so. The man was bigoted, it is true, but he acted in a foolhardy fashion. There were a dozen ways in which he could have shown his contempt for me without encouraging physical retaliation . . ."

"Excuse me."

Kane turned at the touch on his arm. The man facing him was lean as a hound and dressed in a suit that had gone out of style two years ago. He looked familiar–Kane placed him as one of the spectators at his GalTac match.

"My name is Cyrus Archbold. I watched you play today and you were quite good. Who was your tutor?"

"You're very kind. I picked the game up on my own."

"Indeed." Archbold delicately arched an eyebrow.

Kane hadn't meant to sound so offhand, but in truth it had not been difficult. Aided by a near eidetic memory, he had picked up GalTac in five days of watching at the casino.

"I would be honored if you would favor me with a match," the thin man said.

"Certainly." Kane did not see Pendrake's frown of warning.

"Splendid. How about ten thousand a light?"

Kane's mouth went dry. He knew with awful certainty that he was drunk and a damned fool, but there was no way out. He nodded.

"That's settled then. Shall we say tomorrow at eleven?"

Pendrake cleared his throat as the man withdrew.

"Don't say it," Kane muttered. "He's a green patch?"

"Red. A grand master–I've seen him play. It was gauche of him to challenge you."

Kane groaned. "I'll have to throw the game quickly, before he starts doubling."

Pendrake looked at him shrewdly. "Elias, I do not think you will throw the game."

"Why do you say that?"

"I watched you during the match with Mr. Hogate. If you will pardon me for becoming personal, I think gambling is very important to you."

Kane suppressed a stab of irritation that somehow got through the booze and the lingering flush of his GalTac victory. "Not really," he said. "No more than for anyone."

"When I was learning to read your language," Pendrake said, "I came across one of your sayings: 'Everything is sweetened by risk.' "

"That's true enough."

"But only for a few. Most people, indeed most beings I have encountered, shun risk. I do not believe you shun risk, Elias. Perhaps you even seek it out."

When Kane did not reply, Pendrake added, "But perhaps I am mistaken."

"There's another bar, one level up," Kane said. "Shall we give it a try?"

At eleven the next day Kane put up a fight which his opponent was well nerved enough to permit well into the quintupling stage. When the jeweled teeth clattered their eulogy and the attack and defense boards winked the final time, Kane was left without a single credit. He congratulated Archbold and moved away from the GalTac table as quickly as etiquette would allow, pacing over to the transparent dome and staring out at the choppy gray waters of the Atlantic. So this time the trap had closed. Why then did he feel nothing; nothing but a slight queasiness and the certainty that, had he possessed it, he would have blown away twice the fortune he had just lost to Cyrus Archbold?

The rental on the suite ran out at three o'clock, just time enough to clear out. Pendrake accompanied him in discreet silence and, as soon as they entered the suite, began putting Kane's clothes into the suitcases that still smelled of new leather.

"What are you doing?"

"The wrinkles in the back of your suit suggest a deficiency in packing technique," Pendrake replied. Kane tried to peer over his shoulder at the suit. "However, you still have the wardrobe of a gentleman and possibly one of the best valets in the world."

"Damn it, I've got no use for a valet."

Pendrake smiled and pulled open the second suitcase.

When they reached the hopterdock, the sun was down and the landward sky was fading into hues of red and plum. Darkness pushed at the hazy glow of the dock lights and the sea slapped restlessly below as Kane forced himself to consider the humiliation that lay ahead. After the inheritance, he'd not bothered to clear his bank card for credit; he would have to ask Pendrake for cab money to get them to shore. The alien moved up beside him and lowered the baggage to the dock.

"Shall I arrange for a hopter?"

Kane started to answer, then noticed someone leaning against the dock rail a short distance away. A stiff breeze laced with salt and kelp whipped her black hair back but she faced the wind boldly, inhaling with obvious pleasure. Turning, she caught Kane admiring her and returned his gaze—coolly at first, then with a trace of smile. Kane smiled back and walked over to her.

"You're Elizabeth Tyson."

"Don't introductions usually work the other way?"

"Sorry. I'm . . ."

"Elias Kane. And that's your manservant, Pendrake. Don't look so surprised—you're both the gossip of the casino. Hogate's bet was unusual even in this circus."

Kane motioned for Pendrake to join them. "Your coziness with the Chirpones must have made you an even hotter item."

She shrugged. "I'm handling their contract with the casino for the Shul-Rubid tri-d device."

"The Shul-Rubid . . . ?"

She eyed him sharply. "Did you just come off ice?"

Kane shook his head. "I'd like to meet them—the Chirpones."

She looked back out to sea and for a moment Kane thought he'd been dismissed. When she spoke her voice was low and edged with strain. "I could arrange that. Why don't you and Pendrake meet me for dinner tonight? Perhaps I could get Hysrac to join us—he's head of the trade delegation."

Kane tried not to show his disappointment. "I'm afraid we have to leave the casino—urgent business."

"You work in mysterious ways, Mr. Kane. Perhaps another time, then. I'll be returning to New York soon." She swept by him without saying good-bye and disappeared into the casino as Kane stared after her. *You work in mysterious ways, Mr. Kane.* He felt Pendrake watching him.

"What is the Shul-Rubid tri-d device?"

"It is an entertainment form, Elias; easier seen than described. The Chirpones have acquired it from a race no one has yet seen and are offering it as a trade item." The alien studied him. "Perhaps you can see her again in New York."

"Was I that obvious?"

"She is known as a beautiful woman, Elias; though I find her too small and entirely too skinny."

Kane's jaw dropped and then he laughed. It was a good laugh and he felt better afterward. Pendrake smiled tolerantly and waited until Kane finished. "Shall I call a cab now?"

It was like a dash of cold water; Kane chewed his lip a moment. "I don't know how to put this . . ."

"But you are without funds."

"Broke, yes."

The alien's black eyes grew sober. "And I spent the last of my allowance from Mr. Hogate on a tip for the bellman."

"Allowance? I thought Hogate paid you a thousand credits a month."

"No, Elias. He provided room and board, of course, and tip money when we traveled. I'm afraid the arrangement he made with you was based on his desire to avoid public embarrassment." Pendrake brightened. "Tomorrow is the fifteenth—wage day. The thousand credits should be moved to your balance then according to the agreement logged into the betting console."

"Moved to *my* balance?"

"Surely you did not expect Mr. Hogate to pay the money directly to me—a creature."

Kane made a face. "That leaves us standing on the dock all night."

"I couldn't help overhearing."

Kane and Pendrake turned as a short fat man stepped out of the shadows at the edge of the dock. The alien's mouth became a thin line.

"Hello, Hogate," Kane said. "What are you doing out here?"

"Eavesdropping, I fear." The steel magnate addressed himself solely to Kane. "I watched you get cleaned out by Archbold. He's one of the best."

Kane waited.

"I admire a man who would bet his last sou. Please accept my personal cab. I'll take you to shore with my compliments."

"I couldn't . . ."

"I really do insist, just so you'll know there's no hard feelings."

"That's very generous of you," Kane said stiffly. "I'll credit your account tomorrow."

"You'll do nothing of the kind." Hogate took Kane by the arm and ushered him to a berth farther down the dock. Pendrake followed at a distance with the luggage. The wind rattled the collar on Hogate's jump suit and etched foam on the water in the circle of light below the dock. They boarded the craft and Kane settled back into the webfoam, letting the thrust of liftoff press him back gently. What a shambles, he thought, watching the dome fall away and shrink to a spark on the velvet sea. Pendrake sat quietly in the next seat, his eyes points of reflected green from the instrument lights. Kane shook his head.

"This seems out of character for a man like Hogate. . . ."

The hopter coughed, began to whine, and was buffeted by a series of bumps, as though they were skidding across a giant washboard. The pressure of the seat slackened for a moment and sweat slicked the armrests under Kane's palms as his stomach pressed upward against his diaphragm.

"Get your head down," he shouted. "We're going to crash."

Chapter Two

The hopter planed into the ocean, skipped once and settled. Kane stripped away the crash webbing as it began to dissolve and glanced at Pendrake.

"You all right?"

The alien nodded.

"The flotation chambers should . . ." Kane trailed off as he saw the water swirling already past eye level against the dome. The door should have opened after impact; when he tugged the manual latch, it snapped off in his hands. He stared at it stupidly while the ocean closed over their heads. Sensing Pendrake's silence, he turned. The alien was rigid in his seat, still draped in the residue of the crash webbing. His eyes stared with the blankness of a trance—or shock.

"Snap out of it." Kane leaned over and slapped Pendrake. The alien didn't blink; his skin felt like cold dough. Cursing, Kane turned back to the jammed door, groping over every inch of the seam.

He got his breathing under control and settled back to consider their situation. Another hopter might have been near enough to see them crash and sink. Rescue might be on the way. He searched the memory images—the black sky, wind-scrubbed clean of clouds, the mass of the shore, the stars. There had been no other hopters.

A sand shark nosed into the muddy glow of the emergency lighting and inspected him through the dome with its tiny eyes. Kane made shooing motions but the shark stayed, nuzzling the plastite with its snout. Rummaging under the seat, Kane found the tool kit, shoved a pry bar into the seam by the latch and pulled until lights danced at the corner of his eye and he had to think to remember what he was doing. The air tasted like tin.

"Elias."

"Huh?"

"Breathe deeply and be ready to swim. No—do not talk."

The alien crawled over him, slid fingers into the gap left by the pry bar and braced one foot against the back of the cab. With sudden clarity Kane realized that Pendrake must have gone mad—the trance state was a catatonic prelude.

"You can't . . ."

Muscles swelled on the alien's back and arms and his tunic snapped tight. The ocean drowned out the screech of metal and pinned Kane against the far wall, while the instruments sparked and the cab went black. Somehow his boots were off and something tugged his arm and he bumped the door hard going out. Then he started kicking and hoped he was going in the right direction. His heart hammered and his lungs began to hurt. A hard shape bumped against him and he remembered reading how when a shark hit you all you felt was a blow. But his legs still seemed to be kicking, his arms pulling at the water. Finally his head broke the surface. A wave slapped him and he gagged on a throatful of brine.

Don't blow it now, he told himself. Get the legs working again, that's it, and onto your back. So cold. Were his legs working? He could hardly feel them. Water splashed nearby, a more rapid rhythm than the rolling sea. He turned his head and saw Pendrake dog-paddling toward him over the crest of a wave.

"The door—neat trick," he gasped and swallowed more water.

"Quiet," the alien cautioned. He bobbed up and down searching for a while, the moon silver on his slick hair, while Kane concentrated on staying afloat.

"There," the alien said, pointing. "Shore."

They swam for a while until Kane realized that his arms and legs were gone. But his body seemed warm and even the choking draughts of water which came more and more frequently failed to disturb him. Then pebbles scraped his back and the surf pounded in his ears.

Pendrake worked on his arms and legs until the bite of returning circulation roused him enough to sit up. Annoyed by their intrusion, a gull wheeled and scolded above them and somewhere down the beach lights came on and a dog began barking.

"Pendrake." His voice was hoarse; a whisper barely audible above the surf.

"Rest, Elias. Do not try to talk."

"How did you do that—open the door like that?"

"It is a Cephantine meditational technique."

"Could you teach it to me?"

"Possibly, but your calcium-based bones would probably snap under the increased muscular strain."

"Your bones are different?"

"They are based on iron, Elias."

Kane grunted and listened to the waves while an ugly thought worked its way to the surface of his mind. "Do you remember the terms of Hogate's wager?" he said at last.

The alien stared thoughtfully at the breakers and Kane noticed that his ear lacked the cartilaginous ridges found in humans.

"That he would deliver me to you and pay a thousand credit salary each month . . ."

"For as long as we both live," Kane finished.

A day and a half later, Kane was no less chilled by the thought that Hogate had tried to kill him than he'd been that first moment of realization on the beach. Now, as he stood at the guardhouse of the Imperial Security headquarters in New York, waiting for the man inside to get off the vidphone, Kane probed his feelings again. The anger was still there, of course, and the fear, and something else—a manic sensation not unlike what he'd felt at the GalTac boards and gaming tables of the casino. *What's wrong with me?* he wondered. *Am I really always trying to lose it?*

"State your business please." The gruff voice jerked Kane back to reality.

"Elias Kane to see Commissioner Tulley."

"The commissioner?" The ImpSec guard eyed Kane's stylish magenta skin suit and reached reluctantly for the vidphone. "When's your appointment?"

"I haven't got one, but he'll see me."

"Nope." The guard's hand halted on the signal-board. "The commissioner sees no one without an appointment."

"We went through orientation together," Kane lied. The guard's face twisted thoughtfully and he punched a number on the vidphone. As he waited, Kane cleared his mind of his earlier thoughts by inspecting the windowless monolith of the ImpSec building, only half-laughingly referred to by most citizens as the Bastion. Letting his eyes search vainly for a hold on the smooth featureless plastone, he calculated how many days Pendrake's thousand-credit stipend would last them. He smiled as he remembered the alien's indignation at the Bronx flophouse in which Kane had left him to unpack. Being Hogate's manservant hadn't been easy, but at least the man had lived in proper style.

The guard turned back to him with an ingratiating smile. Within five minutes he stood in front of the chrome desk and faced the ImpSec commissioner for the eastern sector of the country. The clatter of office machines in the commons area outside barely penetrated the plastite door of the office. Tulley stood, revealing a stomach gone to flab, and rounded the desk to shake hands with Kane.

"You look prosperous, Elias. I see you haven't changed—telling whoppers to the guard." He laughed a bit too heartily and eyed Kane's clothes.

"I needed to see you, Clay."

"You mean this isn't for old times' sake?"

"I'm here to see *ImpSec Commissioner* Tulley."

Tulley pinched the bridge of his beaked nose between thumb and forefinger and nodded as Kane studied him more closely. He seemed much the same man he remembered from college, except for the loss of hair in front and the gray circles under his eyes—no plastic parlors for Tulley.

"To be candid, I'm relieved that you're here on business," Tulley said. "Things have been hectic."

"The psychopath plague?"

Tulley expelled a gust of air through his nose. "Psychopath plague rubbish. Crime is up and every synpape in the country starts thinking up fancy names for it. It sells papers and gets everyone in a lather, making our job that much harder."

"Then you don't believe it's some kind of mass craziness?" Kane persisted.

"I didn't say that. I believe what my eyes and ears tell me. Come over here a minute." Tulley jerked a thumb toward a wall screen surrounded by rows of switches and banks of microspools. "This piece of tin is the latest Tecton compusayer. It's not one of your ordinary computers—one of these days it'll have my job." Again the forced laugh.

"I beg your pardon, Commissioner Tulley," said a soothing voice from the wall, "but no compusayer will ever replace even the lowliest man."

"It even manages to placate and insult you at the same time," Tulley continued as if he'd not been interrupted. "Sam, would you show us the violent-crimes graphs going back to 2084?"

The screen lit up with a graph of violent crimes over the past five years.

"In 2084," Tulley said, "there were approximately three thousand violent crimes—murder, forcible rape, robbery or assault to kill—per every hundred thousand people in the eastern sector. Roughly the same for the next three years. Then, in August of 2088—

look here—the bleeding thing starts to shoot up. Every damned month, up and up and up, until now we've got fifteen thousand violent crimes for every hundred thousand people. It's the same all over the world from here to Peking."

"Are other crimes up too?"

"Yes, but if you break it out, you find murder taking up a disproportionate share of the increase. That's enough, Sam." The screen blanked out and Tulley sat down heavily at his desk. "I'm telling you, Kane, we've got to get hold of this thing and fast. Sam, there, says we're heading toward total breakdown within a couple of months."

"Seven point eight weeks," the compusayer corrected.

"And the estimates keep getting revised downward." Tulley glared at the screen. "The damned compusayer progressions aren't arithmetic or geometric or anything we can figure out from one week to the next. But one thing is clear: when it does end, there won't be any such thing as human society on this planet. There may not even be any such thing as humans."

Kane thought back over the past week at the casino, his first contact with civilization in nearly a year. There had been signs, incidents, but could things really be so bad?

"By the way," Tulley said, frowning, "you're not working for a synpape, are you?"

Kane shook his head.

"If you are, I won't let you out of here. This has been a talk between old friends and I expect it will remain confidential."

"For God's sake, relax, Clay. I'm not going to do

you in with the press. Now tell me what's behind all this."

"You've just asked the big question. There are plenty of theories; you named one yourself—mass psychopathy. I'm no psychologist, but we've got a few here at the department who are pretty fond of that theory. Trouble is, it still doesn't tell us *why, who* and *how*. Is it the erosion of moral values as the theos are spouting, or is somebody dropping a microvirus into the water supply or slipping it into our wheat pops?"

"You sound like you've considered it all."

"We've worked on everything, no matter how far out."

"What about the colonists?"

Tulley's face became guarded. "That's a possibility, of course. Things haven't gotten any better between the Loyalists and the colonies since this thing started. There are some problems with the theory, like all the rest, but it's currently the Imperator's favorite."

Kane raised an eyebrow. "The Imperator's personally involved?"

"You haven't been listening. Sam gets melodramatic now and then, but I've never known one of his projections to fail. We're in real trouble, Elias. The Imperator has offered a one million credit purse to anyone who can solve the problem."

Kane whistled softly and thought about the money while Tulley flipped a master switch on his desk, shutting down the compusayer. The commissioner eyed his hands with a sly expression. "As a matter of fact, when I heard you were here to see me, the wheels began to turn. We were a good team in college, Elias. We solved some knotty mock-ups together." Kane smiled inwardly at the distortion. If Tulley had convinced himself over the years that he had helped Kane solve those exercises in criminology classes, there was little harm in it. "I always said you should have gone on," Tulley continued, "but no, you were off to the Navy for free piloting lessons. You never could settle down."

"What are you getting at?"

"You don't think I've run off at the mouth like this just for old times' sake, do you?" He inspected Kane's clothes again. "I don't know what you're into right now. Maybe you don't need five hundred thousand credits."

"You want a partnership. You expect me to dope out a problem that's got the top management in Imperial Security stumped."

Tulley shrugged. "I've got some ideas, but I need fresh input. You were good, Elias, and I imagine you still are. It's not just the million credits. I've got to get this thing solved. The Imperator's leaning on the president, the president's leaning on the bureaus and the bureaus are leaning on the commissioners."

"And, of course, people are getting killed," Kane added dryly.

"What? Yes, of course." Tulley eyed him thoughtfully and Kane felt a chill. Something about Tulley had changed, as though some vital part of him was missing. Kane tried to remember what it had been like before, recalled the time Tulley had gotten so upset over the murder of a girl—and it was only a fictional problem case. Abruptly, he made up his mind.

"How about it?" Tulley asked. "You'll be given adjunct ImpSec status, of course, and a regular paycheck, though you don't look as though you need it."

"I'll have to think about it, Clay."

Tulley's mouth set into a grim line. "Not too long, old friend. I imagine Sam will have some more depressing estimates for me tomorrow."

"Soon," Kane agreed.

Tulley flipped the compusayer back on with suppressed vehemence. "You came to see me about something else."

Kane nodded. "It's probably related. A few days ago someone tried to kill me." Kane told him about the wager with Spencer Hogate; how the man had insisted that he ride on his hopter, how the door of the craft had sealed and the flotation chambers failed. "The local police refused to press charges when they learned who was involved," he finished. "Said the casino was out of local jurisdiction."

Kane had expected an argument. Instead Tulley laid his palms on the desk in a gesture of finality. "This is a police matter."

"I don't know any police commissioners," Kane said with a wry smile, "and someone Hogate's size takes muscle. Besides, ImpSec can mix into whatever it wants, Clay. I know that."

"With all that's happening, I can't spare even one agent to investigate a mere attempted murder—and I'm not admitting it was anything but an accident. If you want protection, you can always come to work for us. Now if Hogate actually murders you, then you'll have a case."

This time Tulley's laugh was not forced.

When Kane got back to the room in the Bronx, Pendrake was sitting on one of the beds, which sagged nearly to the floor under his weight. He was cradling a sickly potted geranium on his lap; the clothes were neatly hung in the closet and a loaf of bread and some cheese were laid out on the chipped table by the window. Tattered print curtains stirred on a breeze that carried the first chill of autumn.

"Where did you get that?"

"It belonged to a shopkeeper where I bought the food. It was being mistreated and for an extra credit the owner let me have it."

"Mistreated?" Kane suppressed a smile as he noticed the alien's earnest face.

"Yes, Elias. Plants are very sensitive to emotions. This one, while it was watered and fed, was not loved. It was dying, but now it will live."

Kane looked at the massive hand curled around the flower pot and nodded. "I suppose you'll want to take it with you back to the casino."

"Does that mean your friend decided to help us?"

"We're going to help ourselves." He told Pendrake about his meeting with Tulley.

"Our money will not last long at casino rates," Pendrake said when he'd finished.

"One of my most useful graduate school stints was in the field of probability and statistics," Kane replied. "There are some ways to make the odds work for us, but that's not why we're going back."

"Why, then?"

"To give Spencer Hogate another shot at killing us, of course."

Chapter Three

Kane spent three hundred credits on jet fare to Delaware. By midafternoon they were settled in the casino hotel again—a modest two-room suite this time, for which Kane had to advance two hundred credits. Kane napped for an hour and a half, then got up and dressed slowly in a green brocade V-coat and soft leather pants that spilled into loose folds where they tucked into his boottops. Deciding against an early dinner, which might take the edge off his nerves, Kane instead mentally rehearsed the scenario he would try to create in a few hours. By eight o'clock he was prowling the sixth-level gambling floor. Pendrake strolled beside him, hands clasped behind his back, a powerful but benign presence that Kane hoped would counter the predatory ambience he was sure must be radiating from himself.

There was something strange in the way he felt, and for a moment Kane's concentration, which had been growing over the past hour, faltered as he tried to pin the feeling down. There was a keyed-up excitement, a sharpening of his senses, a loss of appetite—all the things he usually felt when he was ready to gamble, but that was it: he was not here to gamble, not in the casino sense of the word. The distinction was fine but it was there. It was the first time he had been on the floor of the casino without any urge to participate. In fact, the games seemed petty to him now, their stakes devoid of challenge. Part of him wanted to look more closely at the new feeling, to explore its meaning, but he forced his attention back to his surroundings.

The perimeter portion of the sixth floor was the part given over to gambling. The curvature of the outside glass wall, together with dividers of platinum inlaid with onyx and silver designs, served to apportion the outer ring into intimate alcoves in which people played cards and socialized over drinks. Kane and Pendrake strolled between green baize stages on which the darkened audience watched their hands act out the scenes cued by the red and black language of the cards. The faces in the shadows interested Kane more than the play; he stopped finally beside a large table at which six people worked at poker while four stood behind and looked on. The clothes of this group were especially fine, the eyes especially bored, the drinks especially in need of refilling. Kane joined the watchers for a time while Pendrake gazed out at a drifting jellyfish lit in hues of blue and pink.

After a short period of observation during which Kane established eye contact with most of the players, he concluded that there was no consistent winner at the table; large piles of chips shifted back and forth with apparent randomness until one of the players, a thin nervous-looking man with the uniformly red hair of a salon patron, shoved his chair back.

"This is getting us nowhere," the man said. "The cards are seeking their own level tonight."

A young woman sheathed in a gown with shifting patterns of transparency eyed Kane, as she had more and more frequently the past few minutes. "Perhaps some new blood?" she suggested.

"Or a new game," Kane countered.

"What do you have in mind?" The way she pitched her voice awakened the nerves in Kane's groin.

"Something all eleven of us can play."

"Really? That many? All at once?"

"I think Reva wants you all to yourself," observed another woman across the table. A large bull-necked man with the hypertensive face of a senior vice-president cleared his throat and started to get up. A casino waiter entered the alcove and Kane seized the moment gratefully.

"Drinks for all these people," he said loudly.

The big man settled back amidst muted murmurs of appreciation. Orders were taken; introductions made. Three were industrialists, one was a criminal lawyer and the rest of the money around the table was rooted in the upper crusts of blue-blood antiquity. Kane looked around for Pendrake; saw that the alien had withdrawn as far as possible into a corner made by sea window and divider.

"Now what is this game for eleven people?" asked the lawyer after everyone was seated around the table and the remainder of Pendrake's allowance—Kane's stake—had been thinned by the barman.

"What I have in mind," Kane said, trying not to show the care with which he chose his words, "is a mental game—one which is ordinarily dictated by chance but which I propose to win from the rest of you by employing certain powers of the mind and of concentration which I possess."

The undercurrent of side conversations died around the table. "How interesting," said one of the women. "Do you claim to be a psychic?"

"I'll let you be the judge of that."

"What's the game?" The bull-necked industrialist sounded skeptical and Kane marked him out as the antagonist he needed to do it right.

"We are all gamblers," he said. "People who play the odds. Suppose I asked each of you to think of a card in this poker deck and write it down on a slip of paper. What would you say the odds were that at least two of you picked the exact same card?"

"Let's see," said the woman who had first spoken to him. "There are fifty-two cards in the deck and ten of us. So the odds of two of us picking the same card wouldn't be very high; about one in five." There was a general murmur of agreement. As Kane had expected, the woman had not said *at least* two, and no one had caught the vital distinction.

"I take it you do mean both value and suit should be the same," the industrialist said, searching for possible deceptions.

Kane nodded. "And what do you think will happen to the odds if I concentrate very hard on a certain card while you are making your selections?" Pendrake turned from the glass and looked briefly at Kane before returning his gaze to the ocean.

"Why, precisely nothing," the industrialist snorted.

"Perhaps you'd be willing to bet on that?"

"Of course."

Kane looked around the circle; saw assent in every face. No one seemed bored any more, and he let it be his justification. "Very well, here's what I propose. We'll play as many rounds as you like. On every round each of you will put up thirty credits and I will match it with a hundred of my own to be divided ten ways if I lose. You must all wait five seconds before writing down your selection each time."

"We pay three to one stakes for a five to one chance at a payoff," said someone in the circle. "Not bad. And you believe that your concentration powers will shift the odds in your favor?"

"As I said, I will leave it to you to judge."

The industrialist drew a cigar from a gold pocket case and puffed it to life. "Sheer rubbish," he said.

Kane took a memo book from his pocket and passed the sheets around until everyone had plenty. He bowed his head and let it come to rest on the tips of his steepled fingers, feeling foolish and suddenly afraid.

What if the thing somehow failed to work, and he went in the hole and the adjudicator was called in and . . . ?

"Shall we begin," he said.

Kane started out with seven hundred credits. He lost the first round. On the second, two people picked the king of spades and Kane's balance rose by three hundred credits. He won the next game and lost the following two, so that after five games his net gain was three hundred credits.

"Luck," huffed the industrialist, and Kane doubled the stakes. He won six out of the next ten games for a profit of 2,800 credits. The silence around the circle became a goad for Kane's nerve as he won seven of the next ten games for a profit of 3,600 credits. When the lawyer laughed shakily and pushed back his chair, Kane's winnings had come to 6,700 credits. It was not very much by the grossly wealthy standards of the casino clientele, but it would be enough for his purposes; he too broke the circle by standing.

"I must confess," he said, "that my concentration is waning." There was a general sigh of what sounded like relief.

"An amazing demonstration, Mr. Kane," said the man with the red hair.

"Yes, quite amusing," the industrialist admitted. "If I didn't know better, I'd swear the odds weren't really five to one. I'd hate to play poker with you."

Kane bowed his acknowledgment and slipped his credit card into the wager box, which had kept a running tally of the stakes. After transfer of funds to his account was accomplished, he excused himself, adroitly missing an attempt by the woman in the transparent gown to get his attention with her eyes. As he left the table, everyone began talking to each other at once.

Pendrake followed him into a corridor leading to the center area of the sixth level. "I'm starved," Kane said. "Let's grab some supper."

"Elias, that was a most impressive demonstration. I was not aware that you possessed psychic powers."

"Nor was I."

"But with odds of five to one . . ."

Kane stopped and turned to face the alien. "I never said those were the odds. The woman in the interesting dress said that."

"Then there has been a deception. Are you not afraid that someone will lodge a complaint?"

"The only deception was worked by ten people upon themselves. If you will recall, I said I would defeat the group with my mental powers, not my psychic powers. When asked if I possessed psychic powers I offered to let them judge for themselves."

A smile played at the corners of Pendrake's mouth. "You must admit, they have judged you as you required."

"They have invented their own explanation to compensate for the failure of their intuitions. The science of probability is deceptive. It often conforms to intuitions, but there are enchanting exceptions. There is no element of the con game in what I did—no shill, no false statements, no sleight of hand."

"Tell me, Elias, if five to one was not accurate, what were the true odds?"

"Exactly $1-(52/52 \times 51/52 \times 50/52 \times 49/52 \times 48/52 \times 47/52 \times 46/52 \times 45/52 \times 44/52 \times 43/52)$."

"And that comes to . . . ?"

"Approximately sixty percent in my favor," Kane said with a smile. Pendrake was silent for a moment as they found a dropshaft and took it up to the fourth level. After they got off, the Cephantine halted Kane with a touch on the shoulder.

"Elias, I know you are eager to get some dinner, but there is a matter which concerns me."

"Go ahead."

"It is Mr. Hogate. I do not know if you were aware, but he was watching us from across the grand foyer when we registered."

"I was aware," Kane said. "So?"

"Do you not feel uneasy being back here? It is not safe."

"That's the point. It's not safe anywhere. If Hogate

means to kill us, he can have it done anytime, anywhere. Here we can come to a clench with the man. Besides, you agreed that Hogate is not acting as he normally would. A thousand credits a month isn't even pocket money to him. There's only one reason he's after us—the plague. He's got it, and he's where we start. He's our laboratory specimen." Pendrake continued to look doubtful and Kane gave the alien's shoulder a comradely squeeze. "Okay, I'm a bit worried too, but let's eat. I panic much better on a full stomach."

Pendrake shook his head. "You go, Elias. I'll tend to our things in the suite."

Kane nodded. "See you later." When he walked into the dining room, someone called his name. He tried to place the voice, but the light was confusing—candles guttered on the tables and threw grids of shadow through overhanging fish nets to dance on the ceiling.

"Over here."

He saw her at a table in the corner, half in silhouette against the colored lights which warmed the ocean at her back. She was alone except for a wine steward who hovered nearby. Kane made his way across the room and stood in front of her table. "Hello, Ms. Tyson."

"Sit down, sit down."

Kane did as he was told.

"You were supposed to get in touch if you got back to the casino before I left."

"We just checked in a few hours ago."

"And came straight here looking for me so that we could have dinner."

There seemed to be more than jest in her words; he couldn't tell what. "Something like that."

"Good." Her laugh was low and pleasant. "I'm having the crab imperiale. Do you know what you want yet?"

Kane selected Maine lobster and ordered a dry dome-grown Martian wine.

"I'm glad you came back," she said after the steward had glided off. "Rumor has it that you almost got crimsoned." Kane thought about the red mark that went under a person's name on the computer printouts after he'd died, so that the paper man could not outlive the flesh.

"I tried to swim to shore on a bet," he said. "Took out a liter of sea water."

"Don't be flippant. The police were here the morning after you left making polite inquiries of Spencer Hogate. Seems his personal hopter mysteriously dropped into the ocean with two passengers aboard. One of them was two-plus meters tall and pumpkin-colored."

"How did Hogate take it?"

"Oh, he was most distraught."

Kane nodded and looked out into the water. The yellow and blue lights caught each mote and transformed the murk into a dazzling mist through which a school of sea bass drifted.

"It's this thing that's happening, isn't it?" Beth said, leaning toward him. "This mass craziness. I supppose it'll get us all before it's through." She gazed into her wine, her face set as though by a sudden decision. "You're a strange one, Kane."

"What do you mean?"

"You have almost no record in the computers, except a bunch of academic entries—psychology, statistics, criminology, physics, biology—but no advanced degrees. A stint in the Navy where you learned to pilot the paradoxical ships, and became skilled at unarmed combat, and several years during the last ten in which you don't show up at all, not even to charge a hot dog at Macy's. Then, suddenly, you end up here with a small fortune, supposedly inherited, double it on Hogate's tab, then blow it away on a GalTac grand master as if having it around embarrassed you."

"I hope you didn't overpay the private detective."

Their waiter pushed up a silver cart, tied a bib around Kane's neck and began loading their table with steaming dishes. They ate in silence for a while, then she looked at him. "Who are you, Elias?"

"I'm what I seem to be. Why do you care?" He asked it grudgingly, not wanting an answer; wanting to believe that she was attracted to him and not to some mystery she had concocted to amuse herself.

"Because I think I know who you are. You are an agent of the Imperator's Special Branch, investigating the psychopath plague. I suspected it when you first approached me and showed such an interest in the Chirpones—tried to use me to get to them."

Kane frowned. "And what if I was an agent?"

"Listen to me. It's not the Chirpones. You've got to stop badgering them."

Kane's mind clicked, began to race.

"I was threatened with some pretty vile things if I let this out," she continued, "but since you're who you are it hardly matters. Two other agents were in my office three weeks ago, bothering me about them, demanding that I arrange for translator devices so they could interrogate them—but you know all this. Hysrac became so upset that he nearly catabolized."

"Hysrac—that's your Chirpone supplier of the Shul-Rubid device?" Kane remembered their short conversation on the hopterdock.

"That and all the other things they import for trade. You needn't pretend that you don't know."

Kane toyed with a piece of lobster on his plate. So the Imperator's Special Branch was investigating the Chirpone traders, using the aliens' principal human business contact. The situation would be delicate: it was impossible to understand Chirpone speech without an earplug translator; the aliens controlled the translators and enjoyed protected diplomatic status as well. But why were they being investigated? Tulley had said nothing about suspecting the Chirpones; but then, Tulley would not have told him anything important, even assuming the commissioner was privy to the Imperator's Special Branch—not until Kane agreed to a partnership.

"Leave them alone. They're not like us. They're peaceful, delicate creatures. They risk death just by being among us."

"You sound very sure about them."

"If you knew them as I do, you'd be sure too."

"I want to know them. I'll give them every consideration; in fact, you can be with me whenever I speak to them."

Her eyes registered surprise. "You would permit that? The others insisted on a private grilling, yet you offer to let me be present. Why?"

Kane shifted uncomfortably in his chair. "Let's just say that my methods are different. Besides, you know more about them than I do. It's only logical that I work through you." Things were happening too fast, he knew. He needed more information, more time.

"I suppose I haven't much choice. At least this way they'll have some protection. When do you want to see Hysrac?"

"Let's take things slowly. The agents three weeks ago alarmed Hysrac; I don't want to do that." He paused, met her gaze and decided. "Before we go any further I want to clear something up. I am not an imperial agent."

Her expression did not change. "Then how do you explain all those odd facts—the generalized training in just those areas which would be useful to an agent? Nobody else would do that—you've got to specialize to survive in this age. You show no steady employers in your history either. Odd jobs while you were at school. An academic career that just doesn't make any sense. Really, Elias, five different graduate schools? I keep asking myself who would want to study in five of the country's most prestigious doctoral programs without caring that he never got an advanced degree."

"Who says I don't care?" Kane said. "It hurt more each time they flunked me out."

"No school ever flunked you out. Three of the program directors begged you to stay, but you left anyway. Always on to something else. When you were through with graduate school you did that short stint in the Navy—just long enough for you to become a pilot. Not to mention those unexplained gaps in your record—gaps like you'd expect for an agent on mission. Then you show up here just when I and the Chirpone contingent do. I was expecting someone like you after the other agents made such a hash of things. When I approached you last week, you couldn't duck out fast enough. The others made a frontal attack and Hysrac went to pieces, so they send in an anonymous man with the smooth touch—a man good at staying under cover."

"I am not an imperial agent."

She sighed and leaned back. "All right, Elias. Let's agree to something. I'll help you, but you mustn't lie to me." Kane tried to speak and she held up her hand. "No, I accept your position. Let's agree that we won't discuss it again."

Kane shook his head but said, "All right."

She pushed back from the table. "I'm going up to screen a new tri-d and then Hysrac is stopping by to see if I like it. Do you want to come along?" Her voice was cool.

Kane looked at her a moment, then nodded and stood. The casino theater was empty and dark when they got there. Beth turned the lights to dim, walked to the front and activated the olive-colored box that was sitting on the stage. They sat down together in the middle seats and then the stage dissolved and they were looking into a round high-ceilinged chamber in which manlike creatures with wings were soaring in intricate patterns. Some of the creatures were dressed in red and others in iridescent green. From the middle of the domed ceiling hung a golden ball suspended on an elastic cord; at intervals one of the birdmen would swoop and strike the ball, driving it toward silver or black discs that were spaced around the walls of the chamber. Other birdmen would try to intercept or block the ball. The three-dimensional illusion was perfect.

"It's a Tirang match," Beth whispered. "One of the

favorite sports on Sirion V—a planet within the Shul-Rubid confederation. At least that's the explanation that the Shul-Rubid survey mission gave Hysrac when he traded them some Krythian relics for this consignment of cubes."

"Cubes?"

"Yes, that's what goes into the box to produce the shows." She continued to speak softly, as though to avoid disturbing the contestants. "The cubes are made from an alloy of Earth analogue elements. Somehow or other, and nobody's quite sure how, the visual information is coded onto the cubes and transmitted without external light or moving parts. The sound track is much simpler—it resembles our conventional votapers and is keyed to the visual signal."

The action had heated up; some birdmen from both sides were diving at each other and the ball, while others held back and guarded their respective discs. When the ball would strike a disc, a bong would sound and alien script would flash on a circular board in the floor. Kane looked at Beth out of the corner of his eye; she was observing the action with a frown of concentration. Occasionally she would write something in a notebook. He drew in a breath and savored the faint scent of her, wondered how her skin would feel. Abruptly the tri-d ended, leaving the theater again in dim light.

"Interesting." She made a few final scribbles in the notebook and turned to find Kane gazing at her. "What did you think of it?"

"What did I think of what?"

She smiled. "I think I should turn the lights up." She walked to the front and Kane blinked as the lights came on. He walked down the aisle toward her, stopped and turned as the doors at the back opened.

A tall violet-skinned Krythian entered, his hand on the butt of his blaster. Two more Krythians followed him in and looked around, eye-stalks swiveling. Kane studied the bodyguards. They were approximately as tall as Pendrake but their slender bodies were in sharp contrast to the Cephantine's bulk. Their knobby joints and enlarged hands and feet made them seem like gangling adolescents. Rumor said they were deadly shots with the needle-nosed blasters, though, and there was a dull competence in the way they searched out possible danger in the room. When the Krythians were satisfied that the room held no danger, they stood aside and one of them held open the door. A short plump Chirpone whom Kane remembered from his last trip to the casino waddled through, made his way down the aisle and stopped about three meters away, guards flanking him closely on either side. The Chirpone held up a hand in greeting. Beth drew two earplug translators from her purse, installing one in her ear and handing the other to Kane.

"Gweetings, Elizabeth." The voice was high but mellow; the lisp somehow added to the already comical air of the Chirpone and Kane suppressed a smile.

"Hello, Hysrac. May I present a friend of mine, Elias Kane."

Kane stepped forward and held out his hand. The alien shrieked and stumbled backward in terror. The two Krythians who had been standing on either side of Hysrac leaped forward. Each thrust out one arm, striking Kane on either shoulder and tumbling him backward to the carpeted floor of the theater. Kane rolled and sprang to his feet; Beth grabbed him around the shoulders from behind.

"Elias, please!"

The Krythians aimed their blasters at his face. Hysrac recovered himself and held up both hands. "Kaaman, Kaarth," he hissed. "Easy."

For a moment they stood in tableau—Beth clinging to Kane, the two Krythians still as lizards, the Chirpone's hands raised as if to ward off evil. Then Kane felt some of the anger drain out of him.

"That wasn't necessary," he said.

Elizabeth let loose and straightened her halter in sudden self-consciousness.

"I wegwet the incident." The Chirpone's voice trembled and he brought it under control with a visible effort. "My pwotectors are much too zealous at times and I'm afwaid I must accept wesponsibility for that." Hysrac said something to the Krythians; they holstered their blasters and stepped back. Their round fish mouths revealed no expression, however, and their eyes never left Kane's face. "I should not have pwesumed that all humans are aware of the danger they pose to us," the Chirpone continued. The way he said it made Kane feel as though Hysrac had just numbered him among the pitiably ignorant. He searched his memory for details about the Chirpones. As always, his recall was perfect, but there was an information gap left by his solitary year in the desert. Up to the time he had left for that year, the alien traders had made only a few contacts with Earth since the discovery of their planet, Archepellan, by a colonist survey ship six years earlier. They had brought curiosities, exotic foods, plant life, such as the beautiful musal trees, and art objects, all of which had enjoyed a successful market. Their business during these occasional visits had been carried out quickly, and the actual physical details had been handled by Krythians while the Chirpones remained in the ships and communicated with their buyers through remote audio hookups. This had earned the traders a reputation for timidity and had resulted in very little being known about them. The first humans to see Chirpones, a party of survey planetologists from Alpha Centauri IV, knew more about them than anyone else. Their ship had developed trouble off Archepellan and they'd crash-landed on the uncharted alien planet. Later accounts of that first contact were sketchy; Alpha Centauri was the oldest and most independent colony outside the solar system of Earth and recognized no obligation to share information with the mother world. The only other possible source of knowledge about the Chirpones had been the Krythians; however, attempts to question the bodyguards about their employers had been met with silence—it still had not been established whether the Krythians were even capable of speech. Kane did recall a *Journal of Xenobiology* speculation that the Chirpones suffered from some form of social phobia. Eventually trade grew to the point where the Chirpones could no longer conduct business from their ships. More than this mixture of speculation and fact Kane did not know. Now that his anger had cooled, he hoped his ignorance had not cost him too much.

"It was my fault," he said. "I've been out of touch with developments on Earth for a year."

"You are a colonist?"

"No." Kane could feel Beth watching him; he

glanced at her, caught her enigmatic smile. "I've been in a remote place cut off from normal news sources. I wasn't aware of your aversion to being touched."

"I'm afwaid it's more than an aversion, Mr. Kane."

Beth was frowning now. "Elias, surely you know why the Chirpones must avoid all human contact." Kane started to reply but Hysrac interrupted.

"Perhaps it would be best if we show wather than tell your fwiend. The casino has a libwawy, does it not? Perhaps you would like to accompany us there."

Kane felt irritated; wondered why. "All right."

The library was a small but well-equipped room on the seventh level. The air conditioners hummed continuously in deference to the computer which ran the length of one wall. On closer inspection Kane saw that it was not a computer but one of the more sophisticated compusayers, like the one in Clayton Tulley's office. The party had the library to themselves; Kane walked over to the row of seats facing the compusayer and sat down. Beth joined him, while the Chirpone and his bodyguards stood just inside the door.

"If you will ask for the lead video of any major synpape on July 2 of this year, you will see why we bwought you here, Mr. Kane."

Kane wondered if the alien was deliberately patronizing him; he said nothing. After a moment Beth addressed the compusayer.

"NBS lead story, July 2, center screen video, please."

"At your service." This compusayer spoke with a clipped female voice. The screen lit up with a city scene which Kane placed after a moment as being on the old United Nations Plaza in front of the former

Assembly Hall, which was now the Planetary Trade Center. A crowd of reporters was clustered outside the trade building waiting, according to the commentator, for a contingent of Chirpones to emerge. A door opened and four Krythians stalked out and eyed the crowd, which was also being tended by uniformed cops. Finally, the bodyguard escorted three Chirpones to a cordoned area on the plaza where a newly planted musal tree stood waiting. The ribbon around its trunk looked dull in comparison to the maroon blossoms.

"We had been given the key to the city in a cewemony earlier in the day, and were weturning the honor by dedicating a gift of one of our sacwed food twees," said Hysrac, supplementing the steady flow of the commentator. "This is only the second time we'd left our ships."

The three Chirpones were descending the steps toward the cordoned area now, the reporters were pressing dutifully against the police lines and the police were, with tired eypressions, pushing back. Suddenly a man leaped out from between two police, eluded a surprised Krythian bodyguard and grasped one of the Chirpones by the hand. The alien's mouth flew open in a silent scream, its body toppled rigidly and the man backed away looking stunned. Kane watched, hardly breathing, as the synpape camera covering the event zoomed in on the fallen alien. The creature's face was frozen in agony; vapor began to curl from his body, and the outline of stubby arms and legs melted and flowed like wax. Within seconds there was only a pile of dissolved flesh and bone on the pavement. The next moments were a frenzy of confusion as the camera wobbled and panned wildly.

The Krythians closed into a tight circle around their employers. For a second the camera caught sight of the man who had touched the Chirpone. He was running from three cops; they disappeared around the corner of a building and the camera returned to where the two Chirpones were tenderly shifting the remains of their comrade into a shroudlike bag. The Krythians were facing outward, blasters swiveling. The red face of a cop loomed in front of the camera and the tape ended abruptly. Silence filled the library as the two humans continued to view the blank screen. When Hysrac finally spoke, his voice was soft.

"So you see, Mr. Kane, we have had to be vewy careful. We foolishly permitted our wish to expwess fwiendship to wesult in the death of one of our most tweasured associates."

"Was the man ever caught?"

"No," Beth said. "He managed to get away and was never identified."

"It doesn't seem possible," Kane said slowly. "How could our mere touch be fatal to you?" He swiveled in his seat to face Hysrac.

"That is a difficult question for me to answer in your terms," the alien said. "To understand my answer, you must understand how diffewent in certain ways we are fwom you." Hysrac indicated a lounge area in one corner of the library; Kane and Beth walked over and sat down as two of the Krythians pulled a chair back to its maximum distance within the lounge and positioned themselves on either side. Hysrac clambered into the chair and sat with his short legs out in front, like a child.

"We are," he began, "a wace of cowards. I tell you this without shame or apology; in our vocabulary cowardice bears no connotation of disgwace as it does in yours. Our instinct of self-pweservation over the centuwies has been wooted in fear so deep that we will litewally pewish fwom the emotion if it is overexcited."

"But surely you must realize," Kane put in, "that we mean you no harm."

"The importance you assign to intentions is a mystewy to me and my people."

"What do you mean?"

"You humans appear to believe quite persistently, and in the face of much contwawy evidence, that you contwol your actions pwincipally thwough your thoughts. For example, if you do not feel malice toward me, you will confidently assure me that you will not hurt me. In the vewy next moment, the situation might change—the external conditions which forever impinge on all beings may shift in some way outside your contwol and you might leap at my thwoat."

"That hardly seems likely."

"Perhaps; perhaps not. The point is that the major contwolling influence is not your intentions but, wather, the physical, emotional and mental enviwonment which continually shifts and flows awound you. And yet you cling to the illusion of contwol as if your personal worth depended on it."

"Your philosophy is interesting, Hysrac, but it doesn't explain how a human touch can kill you."

"The touch does not actually kill us diwectly. As I said, our instinct for self-pweservation is wooted in cowardice. We invawiably wespond to danger with fear, never with fight or thought. The gweater the danger the more intense the fear. This is automatic—

we exercise no contwol over it. Your species, Mr. Kane, is a dangewous one with a savage wecord which speaks a thousand times more eloquently than your pwotestations of good will, however sincere. Fwankly, we find you quite fwightening. Our tewwor becomes so extweme when you appwoach too closely, that your touch can induce catabolisis–death from sheer fwight. You should be able to understand this. Even your own people have been known to die of fwight."

"Then why do you come here at all?"

"Cowardice is not our only instinct, Mr. Kane. We are twaders by instinct also–it is in our blood. You wepwesent a market, and as long as we are permitted our pwecautions, it is possible to balance the two instincts well enough to deal with you." Hysrac paused and stroked the side of his bill-like mouth as a man might groom his whiskers. "When one does not harbor the illusion of inner contwol over the universe, one finds his pleasure and contentment in being what that universe makes him."

Kane glanced at Beth; felt another stab of irritation at the rapt look on her face. "I appreciate your willingness to explain all of this," he said to Hysrac. "I regret frightening you; I assure you that it won't happen again . . ." He paused and flushed.

"Do not be embawwassed, Mr. Kane. I wespect your sincewity if not your guawantee. I twust that you will likewise not be offended if I continue to maintain the pwecautions which my instincts demand."

Kane nodded curtly, annoyed that the alien had put him so far off balance with his deterministic prattle. Hysrac plopped down from the chair.

"I should vewy much enjoy speaking with you again," he said. One of the Krythians disappeared through the door, then reappeared and motioned. The other two bodyguards held open the double doors and Hysrac waddled through, turning at the last moment. "Perhaps we can discuss the latest twi-d tomowwow, Elizabeth?" She nodded and he departed with a bow.

"What did you think of him?" Beth asked after a silence which Kane perversely refused to break.

"I really can't say yet. There's so much to sift and process."

She appeared satisfied with that. "I think you'll try to be fair with them."

They walked in silence through the hushed curving hallways until they reached her suite. She turned at the door. "Good night, Elias."

"Aren't you going to ask me in for a nightcap?"

She smiled. "I don't think so. Not tonight." Her face shifted to concern. "Elias, what's wrong? Are you sick?"

Seconds passed before he could control his voice enough to force out an answer. "No. It's all right."

"But your face is white; you're trembling."

He twisted his face into what he hoped was a smile, knowing that his eyes were too wide, his teeth too tightly clenched. "I'm just tired. I'll call tomorrow."

She studied him for a moment, then nodded. He held the smile until her door slid shut behind her. Then he expelled his breath and leaned against the wall and tried to understand the feeling that had passed through him when she'd refused to ask him in. The feeling of rage.

Chapter Four

Kane awoke instantly; played back the last few seconds searching for a sound and finding nothing he could identify. He rolled onto his side facing the entrance hall and tried to remember if he had locked the door. He had walked back, lost in thought, from Beth's suite, had mechanically undressed and gotten into bed; nowhere in the hazy sequence could he remember flipping over the manual lock which would have neutralized the print-powered door mechanism. The print lock would open only to his or Pendrake's palm-print—unless, of course, the desk clerk allowed himself to be bribed.

Fabric rustled in the darkness and Kane's hand inched across the sheets toward the light switch. Then he rolled as something smashed down where his head had been. He tried to leap off the bed; got tangled in the blankets and thumped to the floor. Someone dropped on top of him and grabbed for his neck. Kane struck out with the heel of his hand and caught his assailant on the cheek. The man's weight shifted and Kane threw him off just as a light came on. He squinted, caught sight of another man on the other side of the bed holding a short pipe. The first man grabbed at Kane's legs, got one of them and took a short kick on the nose without crying out. Kane dodged as the other man leaped across the bed at him. *Where the devil was Pendrake?*

Both men were now on one side of him; one short and stocky, long arms, thick black hair and eyebrows; the other tall and overweight, broken nose, familiar—he'd stood with Hogate at the gaming tables when they'd arrived back at the casino. The short one hurled his pipe and pain exploded in Kane's ribs; he stumbled backward into the dresser and tried to shout for Pendrake, but the breath wouldn't come. The two men moved in on him.

"That is enough." The alien filled the doorway to the second bedroom. Kane's eyes swam as he blinked and tried to focus on Pendrake.

"Hey, Rolf, he wants us to stop," the big man said with mock politeness.

"Release Mr. Kane. You may take me instead to Mr. Hogate."

"Who said anything about Hogate? Besides, why should we take you for Kane? We've got you anyway."

"Pendrake, for God's sake!"

"I do not think so," the alien said. "You were supposed to kill us both quietly in our sleep, were you not? You have failed."

"We'll get the job done."

"Did Mr. Hogate explain to you that you must kill

us both? If you do not, you will have caused serious trouble for Mr. Hogate. He can be a harsh man."

"Rolf, I'll take this one; you go finish the mouth, there."

Kane tried to react, but the stocky man hit him just beneath the ribs; he didn't remember falling, but raised his head in time to see Pendrake running from the room with both men in pursuit. Kane struggled to his hands and knees and waited for his head to clear. After a moment he was able to stand and make his way to the bathroom. The cold water felt good against his face. Something moved behind him; he whirled and then sagged back against the sink.

"I outran the two men and doubled back here. The door is locked—I doubt they will trouble us again tonight."

Kane stared at Pendrake. The pain in his ribs had begun to subside a little, and careful probing revealed soreness but no breaks.

"You were great," he said sourly. "Those two were remodeling my whole physiology and all you could think of was running away. You could have settled the matter with two swings of your arm."

Pendrake looked ill. "Elias, for ten centuries no Cephantine has used violence against another intelligent being."

"You mean you would not have stopped them from killing me?"

"But I did stop them."

"You know what I mean."

"I have never raised my hand against another intelligent being. If necessary, I would have attempted to restrain the men without hurting them."

Kane shook his head. "They meant to beat us to death—to make it look like we killed each other."

"Fortunately, you awakened in time—Elias, what are you doing?"

Kane pushed past Pendrake into the bedroom, pulled his suitcase from a closet and fumbled at the lining. It popped open to reveal a slim navy-issue needler buried in a recess beneath the false bottom.

"Do you intend to use that on Mr. Hogate?"

Kane withdrew the needler and checked the charge. "You have your values and I have mine. One of mine is to stay alive. Until tonight we couldn't be sure about Hogate. Now we know. Maybe you won't raise a finger to save yourself . . ."

"I value my life very highly, Elias. We can run away—go where Mr. Hogate could never find us."

"Is that what you want? To be hunted across the galaxy knowing every day that someone might blast you from a ventilator shaft, slip a necrinine tablet into your water spigot or slice your spinal cord through the bottom of your mattress?" Kane realized his voice had risen to a near shout. More evenly he said, "It would be better if you went to Hogate right now and bared your throat to him."

"Listen to me," Pendrake said. "You can be thrown in prison for five years just for possessing that thing. Even Hogate's men did not bring weapons such as that one. You are my only friend, Elias . . ."

"I can take care of myself. I'll be back." Kane melded the V-coat seam loosely so that he could get at the gun, then walked out into the hall. His mind was blank as he headed for Hogate's suite. A man stood guard in the hallway outside the suite; he squared around and took a step toward Kane, a blade gleaming in his hand. Kane took out the needler and the man's face went white. The knife dropped on the soft carpet without making a sound and the man raised his hands.

"You are going to open that door for me," Kane said.

The man's Adam's apple bobbed convulsively and his eyes never left the place on the needler where Kane's finger curled around the trigger.

"I can't do that. Hogate will kill me."

"Shall I use this and then put your hand against the panel?"

"No–I'll do it."

"Slow and easy."

The man reached over and placed his palm against the black square. The door slid open and Kane motioned him inside. Hogate was sitting on the edge of his bed; there was a nervag prod in his hand. The two men who'd tried to kill Kane stood stiffly in front of the tycoon. All three turned as the guard stumbled through in front of Kane. Hogate looked at the needler. His mouth opened and closed several times before any words came out.

"Let's talk, Kane."

"You are a dead man," Kane said.

"Now . . . now what will that gain you? You'll get the rope afterward and *you'd* have a lot more time to think about it."

The door behind Kane had slipped shut. Now it flew inward with a crash as it left its runners and Pendrake stepped through. The man named Rolf turned to Hogate.

"You said this one'd be no trouble."

"I said he was a pacifist, you imbecile."

Pendrake bared his arms and the two hit men looked at the round scars. "Is Mr. Hogate preparing your reward for risking your lives tonight?" the alien asked with a glance at the prod. "Do you not worry, Mr. Hogate, that these two may write their own contract?"

Hogate eyed the hit men.

"Stay out of it, Pendrake," Kane said.

"I cannot."

Kane raised the needler to bear on Hogate's head and squeezed the trigger. At the same instant, Pendrake's hand shot out, closing around Kane's wrist and pulling it upward so that the lethal shower of darts buried themselves in the ceiling. Hogate scrambled backward on the bed, his face drained.

"You're hurting my arm," Kane said.

Pendrake let go at once and leaped between Kane and Hogate before Kane could aim the gun again. The millionaire lurched forward and wrapped chubby arms around the alien's waist.

"Stop him, don't let him, don't . . ."

"Move," Kane said. He wished fervently that the weapon in his hand was a blaster set on narrow beam. He could almost see the hand-sized targets weaving back and forth behind their obstructions at the navy firing range. It had been years since he'd taken marksman honors, but the sensorimotor intelligence was still there in his hands, causing his finger to squeeze steadily as he sighted at the quarter moon of Hogate's face, which still showed behind Pendrake's back. He forced the fingers to uncurl again, knowing it was no good—not with a needler. He thought of Hogate's men and glanced to the side, but they had shrunk into a corner and were out of it.

"I believe Mr. Hogate is ready to seal an immediate agreement that for as long as he outlives either of us, five thousand credits a month will automatically go to the survivor, and that for every month he outlives both of us, twenty thousand a month will be deposited to a rival steel combine."

"I said move."

"Yes, yes, I'll do it," Hogate babbled. He peeked out from under Pendrake's arm. "I'll authorize it through CompCentral right now. We can make it a trilateral agreement which can only be revoked by all three of us."

"What good would that do?" Kane snapped. "You'd catch us later and force us to revoke it."

Hogate shook his head. "Perhaps I could break you, but not this one. He'd die first; I know. Besides, once this goes on record, my reputation would be ruined by any action which might draw attention to it. You could take precautions—a hidden explanation to be released if you die. . . ."

"Your reputation," Kane said. He looked at Penrake and knew that Hogate was right about the Cephantine. Something went out of him; the needler wavered and then dropped. "All right."

When they were back in their suite, Kane fell on his bed and tossed the needler across the room. "Get rid of that thing, will you?"

"It will be a pleasure." The alien walked over and picked the gun up by the barrel. Kane watched from the bed as he unloaded it, flushed the needles into the atomic waste chute, then crushed the weapon in one fist.

"Something's happened to me," Kane said.

Pendrake tossed the ruined needler into the chute. "Yes."

"This evening I was with Beth," Kane went on as though talking in his sleep. "When I walked her back to her suite, I wanted to go in for a nightcap and . . . and for whatever else might happen. No, that's putting it wrong. I wanted to go to bed with her. Are you familiar with that euphemism?"

"Yes, Elias." The alien still stood by the waste chute staring at its protective lid, but his attention was entirely on Kane.

"She refused me. It should have been nothing. Hell, ordinarily I wouldn't have suggested it in the first place—it was the first that we'd spent any time together. Not even a date. But when she refused me, Pendrake, I was furious. I even thought of forcing my way in and . . . and . . ."

"Raping her?"

"Damn it, yes. And now, what just happened with Hogate. I don't know why I reacted the way I did; I meant to kill him in cold blood. . . ."

Pendrake looked at Kane and there was sadness in the dark eyes. "It would have been better," the alien said, "if you had not returned to civilization."

"What do you mean?"

"The psychopath plague, Elias. You have it."

Kane had known it already, but hearing the Cephantine say it crumbled his last irrational defense, the remaining forlorn hope that it wasn't true. He felt the blood draining from his face, clutched the bedspread with both hands.

"Elias, you are ill. I will summon a doctor."

Kane struggled to merge the two worried orange faces that hovered above him. "No, don't do that."

He sat up and breathed deeply until he felt less queasy and things were in better focus. "There's no cure for what I've got anyway. What is it, Pendrake? Is it a microbe? A poison? I don't feel any different, but it's inside me somehow. It's real."

"I do not know," the alien said helplessly.

Kane pushed the heels of his hands against his forehead. "I can't think, *I can't think.*"

"Much has happened. You are weary. Perhaps sleep will clear both of our minds."

Kane nodded, but he sat on the edge of his bed in the darkened room for a long time after the alien had retired to his quarters. Finally he let himself quietly out of the room.

The next morning they were awakened by a redcoated waiter, bringing the breakfast Pendrake had ordered the previous afternoon. Kane stared without appetite at the eggs scrambled in cream, the rasher of bacon and the stack of buttered toast. "You should try to eat something," said Pendrake.

"I'll wait until lunch."

The hotel portion of the casino was above water now and Pendrake had drawn back the curtains over their window port to admit a cylinder of morning sunlight. Outside, gulls coasted against a blue sky and dove occasionally into the sparkling water. Kane eased back from the fold-out table next to his bed, ignoring the ache in his ribs, and began pacing to the window and back. Pendrake finished his toast, stacked their dishes on the trays and deposited them in the hall.

When he returned, Kane stopped pacing and searched the alien's face. "What you did last night—you may have to do it again."

"I will help you all I can, Elias."

"For some reason you don't seem to be affected. If you can stand watch on me, maybe we can get through this thing."

"In many ways I am quite similar to your species. It may happen to me soon also."

"If it does, we're really in a box."

"What will we do now?"

"I couldn't sleep after we finally got to bed again so I went to the library and did some research. I scanned digests of everything important to be printed in major synpapes the past three months. Most of it looks like speculation but there are a few things I'd like to follow up. First I'm going to vid Tulley and ask him about the Chirpones."

Pendrake looked surprised. "You suspect the traders of being involved in the plague?"

"The Imperator's Special Branch does." Kane told him how Beth Tyson had mistaken him for a Special Branch operative and why, and concluded with a summary of his encounter with Hysrac. When he had finished, the alien looked thoughtful.

"What were your impressions of Hysrac?"

"He's a bit pompous and more than a little patronizing, but it's hard to see him in any kind of aggressive role," Kane said. "He seems to have a very fatalistic philosophy, and if he's not an abject coward he is a consummate actor. The Krythian bodyguards are more the type for planetary conquest, except they appear to lack the brains for this kind of finesse."

"Planetary conquest?"

"As long as we're thinking about the Chirpones or any other extraplanetary group as possible suspects, we'd have to consider conquest of Earth as the prime motive for what's happening. What better way to take over Earth undamaged and without resistance than to somehow provoke its populace into wiping each other out? When things have fallen into chaos, whoever is behind it merely walks in and takes over."

"But what if there is no intelligent or purposeful force behind what is happening? What if the cause is more diffuse—for example, a general decay in society as some social scientists and theologians have accused, or an attack by some as yet undiscovered microvirus?"

"Those things are possible, of course. If it is some generalized cultural phenomenon, which I doubt because of the rapid onset, then no one will solve the problem in seven weeks. That's all the time we've got according to Tulley's police compusayer, and the estimates keep getting shorter. The microvirus theory and its variations are pretty good, and I'm sure the microbiologists are hot after those avenues. If that's it I hope someone solves it soon, but it won't be us—we don't have that kind of expertise. I think our best bet is to assume that some intelligent force is behind what's happening. If we can find out who, we'll soon know how and why."

"Who, then, are your chief suspects?"

"The Chirpones are a good starting point, simply because Special Branch is interested in them, but it could be another group of aliens. There are lots of races beyond the eight parsec radius of stars our ships have reached. Some of them are undoubtedly more advanced than we are and could have infiltrated Earth without our knowledge." Kane did not voice another thought—that the spreaders of the plague could even be Cephantines. What did he really know about them? Only that he believed the one in the room with him would rather die than harm him. Kane shook off the thought. *There had to be limits.*

"It need not be aliens, either," Pendrake said. "There seems to be considerable acrimony between your own colonies and Earth. Perhaps Alpha Centauri has decided it would like to be the center of the Terran empire and collect the taxes now paid to Earth."

"True." Kane walked over to the vidphone, sat down and tapped out the number of the eastern sector ImpSec bastion. Clayton Tulley's face appeared on the screen. He looked even more haggard than when Kane had last seen him. The circles under his eyes were almost blue and the skin of his face seemed to sag.

"Hello, Kane. Made up your mind about what we discussed?"

"I need information."

"Are you in or out?"

Kane paused. "There's something I have to know first."

Tulley scowled. "Why should I tell you anything?"

"I'm willing to trade information."

"Then you've already been working solo, after picking my brain . . ."

"Hold on, Clay. I've got to get some feel for this thing before I make up my mind whether to join you." Kane knew he should feel guilty.

The commissioner rubbed his eyes. "What've you got?"

"The Imperator has put his Special Branch onto the Chirpones."

"Is that all? You call that information?"

"It's worth what I'm asking."

"I'll decide that. What're you asking?"

"Have you checked out the Chirpones?"

"I told you before, we've checked out anything and everything."

"And?"

"And now you're going into debt. Sure, we've checked them out. We've scanned, deep-probed and irradiated every consignment of goods they've brought in for trade on the off chance there's a little vial of some nasty microbe or some other baddie tucked away somewhere. We've interviewed them. One nearly dissolved from fear right here in my office. We've gotten complete profiles on their culture from our embassy on Archepellan and it's no dice. Dead end; forget it."

"You sound like you really did the job on them."

"Worked 'em over as much as diplomacy would permit for nearly a month—them and all the other alien contingents on Earth. It was one of the first things we thought of when this thing started to break."

"Then why did two imperial operatives get rough with the chief Chirpone rep just two weeks ago? Surely the Imperator has access to your files?"

This time there was a long silence on the other end during which Tulley stared thoughtfully at him. "Are you in or out? I'm not going to ask you again."

"I'm out."

"Why?"

"I'm not sure I can trust either of us."

"What's that supposed to mean?"

"It's started happening to me, Clay, and I think it's affecting you too."

"Good-bye, Kane." The image faded to a dot, then disappeared. Kane stared at the screen for a while.

"Tulley's covering up," he said at last.

"Agreed. Where does that leave us?"

"It leaves us chasing after the Chirpones."

"Because the commissioner is hiding information about them?"

"Partly. Mostly because they're our best guess. There isn't much time. We've got to gamble, and I've got a hunch about them. Something's not right; I can't put my finger on it but it's there."

"They are very shy creatures. It will be difficult getting close enough to them to find anything out."

"We'll find a way; first I want to follow up something I read this morning. There are two men in New York that I want to see. One of them is an old friend who's chief pathologist in the borough of Queens. The other is a crackpot professor at Columbia who just might not really be a crackpot."

Chapter Five

Kane's stomach lurched upward and he considered the symbolic fitness of descending into a morgue. Outside the drop shaft, bars of light flashed upward at a dizzying rate, then slowed as the shell plunged into the basement levels. He was alone; Pendrake had balked at joining him and had instead set out to get them a hotel room. The shell nudged bottom and the gleaming chromalloy doors slid back to reveal Dr. Alfred Li. Kane stepped forward and returned Li's gaze for the short interval both men could tolerate without embarrassment. The pathologist's open lab coat revealed the same slight powerful body that Kane remembered from college days. Li's head, a trifle large for his body, still bore its mane of straight coal-black hair and his eyes the same odd mix of curiosity and caution. A round alarm-bell mechanism dangled from Li's belt and a series of insulated wires ran upward and disappeared under the lapels of the coat.

Kane held out his hand and the pathologist shook it. "I almost didn't recognize you in your white coat," Kane said. "What about all those TV intern jokes?"

"My paisley ones are in the wash." Li's smile was tired.

"How are you, Alfred?"

"If you mean has it affected me yet, the answer is yes. Pardon my bluntness but the times seem to favor it. I've seen Clay's charts too."

"Then Tulley's been talking to you about me."

"Not exactly old school chum gossip, either. He called just after you did. Warned me you'd probably want to consult me. It would appear that he still knows you pretty well after all these years. He said you have no official status or clearance and that I shouldn't spill my guts to you. He never was any good at puns."

Kane frowned. The commissioner had no doubt already consulted Li and knew that Kane was likely to do the same. But why should Tulley want to stop him?

"And how well does he know you after all these years?"

"Not well enough, it seems." Li motioned at a pair of green double doors across from the drop shaft. AUTHORIZED PERSONNEL ONLY was printed on each door in block letters. "Care to get started? I'm afraid they're piling up at the other end."

Kane nodded. Li led him through the doors and into a cold cement-walled room where three pale bodies lay on glistening gurneys. There were two men, one old and one young, and a teenaged girl. The old man bore the characteristic pin-cushion spread of a needler in his left shoulder. There was an ugly red pucker, inexpertly sewn shut, just beneath the girl's sternum; her flesh was the marbled white of exsanguination. The neck of the other male corpse was covered with the purplish red marks of manual strangulation. Water was rinsing from the upper end of his table to wash around the body and gurgle down a drain beneath the rigid feet. Against one wall were shelves lined with brown and clear-glass bottles. Kane caught a whiff of formalin and his eyes began to water. A silent large-boned man in soiled whites—the deaner, Kane supposed—stood at the head of the middle table and waited while the pathologist scrubbed at a sink in the corner. Li nodded at the man and he began cutting at the skull of the younger man with a circular power saw. The blade buzzed angrily as it sliced through flesh and bone, and tiny red flecks began to pepper an already discolored area on the front of the deaner's gown. When the deaner had removed the brain, Li inspected it for a moment, turning it in his hands and sometimes probing gently. When he had finished, he placed the organ in a metal bowl. After a moment a tape curled up and out of a box of sensors and transducers below the bowl and Li read a series of numbers into a mike which hung down from the ceiling. He chalked some figures on a board at the foot of the table while the deaner set to work opening the girl's skull. As he lifted the head to begin his cut, it slipped out of his hand and thumped on the table. The deaner cursed and lifted the head again—by the hair. The brief routine of the autopsy was followed again and for the older man as well, then Li pulled off his gloves with a snap.

"Okay. Sew 'em up and ask Rollie to make up some slides—the usual set from the hypothalamus plus a random longitudinal sampling moving forward from the cerebellum." He turned and Kane followed him through a side door into a tiny office, cluttered with a desk full of slides, path reports and beakers with gray spongy sections soaked in preservatives. An exhaust duct in the ceiling sucked continuously and Kane edged over toward the floral airstick in one corner.

"Not that it matters," Li muttered. "Not that it matters." He plopped onto a bare spot on the desk and pointed out the room's only chair, which was burdened with a box of reagents. Kane lowered the box to the floor and sat down.

"So?" he said.

"So you saw them. The old man was chief teller in a bank—been there for thirty-four years. Suddenly yesterday he comes to work packing a needler, heads for the vaults and shoots it out with the guard. As for the girl, she tried to knife her boy friend because he wouldn't take her to a whiffer party. He snatched the knife away and stuck her instead. He's in one of the holding pens in Central Park waiting for a temporary cell in one of Queens' four emergency jails."

"It's that bad?"

"Worse. The young guy took a chair leg and tried to remodel his neighbor's skull for playing the stereo too loud. The neighbor strangled him and then ran away." Li rubbed his eyes. "Three more dead people who showed bizarre or psychopathic behavior before their deaths. Three brain autopsies and no gross abnormalities except for those directly implicated in the manner of death."

"Maybe the microscopic will show something."

Li shook his head. "No, no it won't. I wish I could

forget how many of these people I've looked at in the last ten months—lots of them acted crazier than these three. Every time it's nothing; no unaccounted for gross abnormalities, no lesions, no microscopic pathology, nothing. Every pathologist who can still pick up a scalpel is working on this. We've run all conceivable tests currently known on these brains. Tulley keeps calling up and bugging me . . ." The bell on Li's belt rang suddenly and he stopped in midsentence and took a number of deep breaths. For the first time Kane noticed the latticework of hair-fine wires which formed a mesh over the pathologist's left palm. After a moment Li smiled, but his clenched teeth ruined the effect. "It's a little device I cooked up," he said in answer to Kane's questioning look. "The mesh here forms a galvanometer and when I start getting too emotional the bell goes off, cuing some posthypnotic meditation. It works most of the time, but I have to turn it off when I'm in gloves, of course, and I did throw a path report at my deaner the other day. Fortunately he's a masochist and I'm a lousy shot. I'm thinking of rigging it to give me a shock."

"You'll become a zombie."

"Better than hacking up some technician with a scalpel." Neither man smiled.

"What about the peripheral nervous system?" Kane said after a moment. "If you're only doing the brains, mightn't you miss something there?"

"It just can't happen that way," Li said. "Oh, we used to do completes when it first started, but then we got swamped and now we only do brains of people who've turned psychotic just before. It's got to be the brain—some test we haven't invented yet, some nook or cranny that we've never doped out. Got to be the brain. Got to be." The pathologist rubbed his eyes again and yawned. The door opened and the deaner stuck his head in.

"Ready with the next three, Doctor."

Li nodded. "When you've got it solved come down again and I'll break out a beaker of C_2H_4OH, and we'll get a start on preserving ourselves for posterity."

"When *I've* got it solved?"

"That's right, Elias. Because if you can't do it, nobody can."

Kane climbed into the hoptercab, instructed the autopilot to fly northwest to Columbia University and settled back to consider the pathologist's last remark. He became so absorbed in his thoughts that he almost didn't notice that he was being followed. Had his eye not been captured by the way the sun danced on the East River and gilded the red and gold foliage of Randall's Island, he might not have seen the shadow of the hopter flit across the treetops directly below. It was still morning, the sun was in the sky behind him; therefore the shadow had not belonged to the hoptercab but to another craft which followed quite close in its wake. The skies of New York were no longer crowded with hoptercabs as they had been fifty years ago, before the first humans had left for the stars. The 930,000 inhabitants of the city who remained hardly taxed a computerized beam network designed to accommodate a population of fifteen million. Consequently, hoptercabs rarely came within a hundred meters of each other. Kane tried to get a fix on both shadows at once but they were already lost in the steel chasms of Manhattan. However, judging from the probable angle of the sun and the size of the shadow, the tailing craft could not be more than fifty meters directly behind. A glance backward confirmed that the other hopter was in the blind spot dead astern, hidden by that portion of Kane's hopter lying aft of the cockpit.

When the hoptercab passed over the sliver of Morningside Park and began to drop onto the university's landing tower, Kane caught one more glimpse of the shadow. He watched out the back as his cab settled, knowing that the other hopter might now have to reveal itself. He saw it for only an instant above the metal horizon of his own hopter's body before it too dropped downward and was lost below the edge of the tower. It was a sky-blue two-seater with the small extra burner which was outlawed on all but police, military and ImpSec vehicles. They had been good, Kane reflected, even daring to drop their own hopter to ground level on the off chance he might be looking out the rear. Tulley was having him followed. Kane put the fact away for slow digestion and climbed down to the roof of the tower where Pendrake was waiting for him.

"Did you see it?" he asked the alien.

"See what, Elias?"

"The other hopter. Tulley's put his hounds onto us."

Pendrake smoothed his long upper lip with all three fingers. "I shall have to be more observant if I am to be of any help to you."

"Forget it. Let him watch. You found a hotel?"

"Yes."

"And the appointment with Dr. Vogelsang?"

The alien looked downcast.

"What went wrong?"

"I am sure he is there, probably in his lab, but his secretary was an elderly and rather embattled-looking individual who refused to let me speak with him. She said that the professor has grown weary of ridicule and now refuses all interviews with the press. I am afraid I was unable to convince her that we are not reporters."

"Where is his office?"

"In the new physics building—that one over there." Pendrake pointed to where a gleaming tower of glass and ceramic-coated steel dominated a cluster of smaller buildings arranged around a xenobotanical garden.

"Let's go."

Pendrake had assessed the woman accurately. She was short and plump; dressed in gray, which matched her hair. She glared at them as soon as they entered the outer office. Kane noted the door at the back labeled KURT VOGELSANG, PH.D., PROFESSOR EMERITUS. The woman got up and moved in front of the door.

"We'd like very much to see the professor . . ."

"As I've already explained to your companion, Dr. Vogelsang is in his laboratory and cannot be disturbed."

"We're not from the synpapes, ma'am. We're here on a matter of great importance having to do with the professor's theory."

"All you reporters are here on a matter of great importance. The professor's been bedeviled enough by you people and those awful men from Imperial Security. His theories are a matter of record and I won't have him disturbed again." She had moved toward them and was actually making shooing motions with her hands when the door behind her opened and a thin man stepped out. Only a few strands of white hair, combed artlessly forward, divided his pink skull, and the eyes which peered from behind his bottle-thick lenses reminded Kane of faded buttons.

"What is it, Emma? Who are these people?"

Kane stepped forward before she could speak. "Dr. Vogelsang, we're here about the psychopath plague and your theory. We'd like to talk with you."

"They were just leaving," the woman said.

"Yes, yes, Emma—you, come over here where I can see you." Vogelsang peered around his secretary at Pendrake, who moved over and offered his hand to the professor. "Ah, a Cephantine. Good, good. I never expected I'd meet one of you. Fascinating."

"The pleasure is mine, sir," the alien replied. "Few know of my people; I am honored that you recognize me."

Vogelsang continued to grip his hand. "Yes, well, it's the fingers, you know. Can't see too well, but you've got three fingers and I haven't lost my color vision. Well, come in. Don't just stand there." He ushered them into his lab; Kane ignored Emma's venomous look and closed the door gently behind him. The lab was a clutter of wires, scraps of sheet metal, a dozen different monitors, some welding equipment and, in the center of the room, a stripped-down hopter chassis. The antigrav pods were missing, but the thrust engines were still intact, and most of the monitors were wired to various parts of the engines. Vogelsang motioned them to a lab bench and pointed in the general direction of two stools. He wiped his hands on the lapels of his smock and peered at the Cephantine. "Well, what was it you wanted to see me about?"

Kane and Pendrake exchanged glances. "About your theory, sir."

"Oh, yes, yes. And the psychopath thing. Are you from the government? I'll have nothing more to do with the government."

"We're not from the government. We'd like very much to hear your explanation of what is causing the plague," Kane said.

"It's in the papes. Those fools at the *Journal of Physics* wouldn't publish it, but I made sure it got into print anyway."

"I'm afraid the synpapes weren't very specific."

"Eh? Of course not. They got it all mixed up—made me look like a dodderer. They laughed, but they're the fools. I'll show them yet."

"I've had some training in physics, Doctor. Perhaps if you explained it to me."

"It's the hopters. I've done the experiments and I'm sure of it. It's actually been with us for years—ever since the old internal-combustion engines. If you had only studied the records the way I have. There were more acts of pure craziness that occurred in those old machines, or just after people had driven them, than can possibly be accounted for by any other theory." Vogelsang appeared lost in thought.

"And what theory is that?"

"Why, the waves, of course. Those engines put out waves that interfered with people's normal mental functioning—isolated them from one another." Vogelsang fumbled around the lab bench until he found a fat, dog-eared notebook. "It's all in here. People getting out of cars and shooting each other, running each other off the road. Risking accidents and death to cut each other off—perfectly mild-mannered normal people the rest of the time. Especially in the cities during what was called rush hour. That's the point. There were high levels of these waves at those times and a corresponding rise in violent and crazy acts."

"You have found evidence of these waves, Dr. Vogelsang?" Pendrake asked.

"Mostly inferential, I admit, but they're there. A whole spectrum of infra and ultrasonic frequencies that were masked from the earlier crude detection instruments by more salient noise. It's just a matter of rooting them out, teasing them apart."

"But people no longer drive cars . . ."

"Of course not, of course not. But it's the same thing with these hopters only much worse. The effects are cumulative, I'm sure of it. Not the antigravs, but the directional drives. Same kinds of waves put out by friction in the rapidly moving parts. And the cockpit acts to magnify these waves and focus them on the driver or passenger."

Kane looked at Pendrake again. "And you say these waves interfere with . . ."

"With brain waves. That's right. Mixes them all up. Keeps people from reacting to each other in normal, rational ways."

"I'm not sure what you mean by brain waves."

"Kirlian auras, young man. There's your evidence."

Kane searched his memory, recalled the quasi-scientific sect of the previous century which had experimented with photographing the random electric spillage of the nervous system. "But, Professor, the notion of electrical auras having any significance at all has been discredited for a long time."

"Bah. They didn't know what to look for. I do. If I

could only get the department to appropriate funds for the construction of a special camera I have designed. And the neurology people—they won't help me either. In the old days, back when I won the prize, they would've. They would've had to, no matter how crazy they thought I was. But now they dismiss me as a harmless old fool. Gave me this lab to putter around in. No real equipment. Patronizing young shavetails. In the old days . . ." Vogelsang paused and looked around in apparent confusion. "But what was it you wanted to see me about?"

Pendrake got up and walked over to the old man, taking his bony veined hand, as Kane watched thoughtfully. It has been a pleasure meeting you, Professor," the alien said gently. "Thank you for telling us your theory."

Vogelsang smiled. "Of course, of course. Never met a Cephantine before. You must come for tea. It's the three fingers you know. My eyes . . ."

Pendrake followed Kane out of the lab and past the scowling secretary. Neither of them spoke until they entered the hopter-tower lift.

"A sad thing, Elias."

"Yes. It's strange . . ." The door slid open to the roof and Kane's next words remained unspoken as he stared back at the frowning face of the ImpSec commissioner for the eastern sector.

Chapter Six

Two agents flanked the commissioner; a black limousine stood in the background, its antigravs still popping softly as they cooled.

"Hello, Clay."

"Elias." Tulley glanced at the Cephantine.

"Oh, you haven't met Pendrake. Pendrake, this is ImpSec Commissioner Clayton Tulley. You remember, my old college buddy." The reminder, spoken to the alien, had its intended effect on Tulley. He smoothed his face with an effort and nodded.

"I am pleased to meet you, Commissioner. Mr. Kane has spoken highly of you."

Kane frowned at Pendrake.

Tulley grunted. "Thought you might like a ride to wherever you're going." He indicated the limousine and they walked across the roof. Kane and Pendrake climbed into the back with Tulley and the two unsmiling agents sat up front. A plastic screen slid up to isolate the passengers in the back and Kane felt rather than heard the directional drives start up. He thought briefly of Vogelsang's theory, then turned in the seat and studied Tulley. Pendrake sat on the other side of him and appeared engrossed with the view as they rose from the roof and swung out over East Side Manhattan.

"Where to?" Tulley asked.

"You mean you're not taking me in?"

"Now why would I do that?"

Kane smiled and turned to the alien. "Where to, Pendrake?"

"The Hotel Alpha."

Tulley pushed the intercom and instructed his aides to circle in the area of the hotel until he gave the order to land. "How is it that your friend knows where you're staying and you don't?"

"As Mr. Kane's manservant," Pendrake put in, "I handle such arrangements for him."

"Does that include answering his questions for him?"

"I beg your pardon, sir." Pendrake turned back to the window.

"A manservant, eh? You have come up in the world, Elias. Can we talk?"

"I trust Pendrake completely."

"I'll come to the point, then. I want you to stop fooling around with this psychopath thing."

"Why?"

"Because I ask it."

"You know I can't accept that, Clay."

"I could take you in."

"So you could. Why don't you?"

Tulley settled back in his seat and pinched the bridge of his nose in the gesture of fatigue Kane knew so well. "You said something on the phone. You said you are affected and that you think I am too. Maybe you're right. We have been friends. I remember that now, intellectually, but it does nothing for me in here." Tulley tapped his chest. "That scares me, Elias. That really scares me. You might say I've finessed myself out of putting you away—for now. I'm second-guessing everything. I only know how I *should* feel; I try to act that way, but the ice is thin, Elias, it's real thin. Don't push me; don't make me mad, I'm asking you."

Kane nodded. "I don't want to get in your way, so why don't you tell me what has you so worried and I'll try to go easy."

"You'll have to do better than that. . . ." Tulley took a deep breath and gazed out his window. Kane looked past him to where the landing platform atop the Alpha swung in circles below them. "There's a lot you could do that wouldn't bother me," Tulley said at last. "But the problem with you is that you won't stop at anything once you get hold of something—not even if I spell out the taboos."

"So give me some hints and I'll at least tread softly."

Tulley sighed. "There are certain parties who have, after very delicate negotiations, agreed to help the World Government with its problem. Their assistance could prove invaluable, but they could easily be persuaded that it's best to remain uninvolved."

"You mean scared off, don't you? Come on, Clay. It's obvious you're talking about the Chirpone traders."

"I said nothing about the Chirpones."

"And I'd swear to it, if anyone asked me," Kane

agreed. "Let me guess. You told your liaison in the Special Branch that I was aware of their attempts to interrogate Hysrac. But the rough stuff's all over now—Special Branch has made a deal with the Chirpones to keep their eyes and ears open on all their trade routes beyond the reach of our ships. Before, when they put the screws on Hysrac, they learned the Chirpones panic easily. That's why they've told you to keep me away from the traders."

Tulley glared at him, but said nothing.

"So I'll go easy. You know me, Clay. I can use the soft touch."

Tulley thumbed the intercom button. "Set it down. All right, Elias, you can go. But remember, I've got you on a short rope. If one of us gets choked it won't be me. Officially you're to give up your investigations. Unofficially, if you put one toe across the line . . ."

The blood rushed to Kane's face. "Don't you push me, either. . . ."

Tulley squared around and the cab seemed suddenly smaller. Kane saw his own strain mirrored in the commissioner's face. "It can't go on much longer, can it, Clay?"

Tulley shook his head. "The compusayer has now revised it to three and a half weeks." The limousine touched down; Tulley opened the door and got out. Kane and Pendrake climbed down and the commissioner jumped back into his seat, made a curt hand motion to the men in front and closed the door without a word. The hopter pulled away and veered in the direction of the ImpSec bastion a few blocks to the north.

Kane turned to Pendrake. "What's this Mr. Kane stuff?"

"A servant should not appear too familiar in the presence of others."

"For God's sake, Pendrake, we threw the damned collar away. . . ."

"Elias, in my culture, serving another is one of the most honorable positions one can have. The brass collar and the treatment accorded me by Mr. Hogate were both gross indignities and I am in your debt for ending them. To serve you is a great honor for me, however, and a prudent idea as well."

"What do you mean?"

"There is currently on Terra an attitude of mistrust for aliens, encouraged no doubt by the troubles your people are experiencing. The servant in your culture is less visible and much less threatening. I think it is best if people view me that way."

Kane grunted but said nothing. When they got to their rooms, the vidphone was chiming. It was Elizabeth Tyson. She was back in New York and she'd called fourteen hotels before finding them and why did they run off so suddenly, and would they like to come to dinner? They went back up to the roof and took a cab to her estate, the former Wolcott mansion on Long Island, as darkness fell.

The house, bathed in pastel lights, sat atop rolling landscaped lawns and surrounded a central garden courtyard. Kane and Beth had Lupian wood fowl dressed with soft bread and plums from Zenaph; Pendrake ate sautéed mushrooms and a large wedge of the bread. Afterward, the Cephantine strolled the estate while the two humans shared brandy in the garden. Crickets chirped a measured autumn prelude and cool winds from the Atlantic set the tops of the taller garden trees to rustling. The yellow globes of a musal tree hung close to Kane and their spicy fragrance mingled with the brandy vapors. Kane reached up and touched one of the smooth globes.

"That would look good in a fruit compote," he said.

Beth smiled. "It might look good, but if you ate it, it'd dim your lights pretty fast."

"Poisonous?"

"To us, very; to the Chirpones it's the staff of life. Hysrac gave me that one to honor our friendship, although I often think it was really so he could have a snack whenever he visits."

"How often is that?"

"Whenever he's on Earth he always comes by several times. He was here earlier today; he's sold out his present consignment and is going back to Archepellan tomorrow."

It was the perfect opportunity; Kane sat forward, suddenly intense. "Can you get Pendrake and me on that ship?"

She stared at him in surprise. "I don't know. It's really too late for you to get the normal clearance from Earth Government—but of course that's not a problem for you. . . ."

"I'd rather Hysrac merely thinks I'm a friend of yours. If you could convince him to request special clearance from emigration authorities . . ." It should work, he thought. Unless Tulley knew about his friendship with Tyson, he'd have no reason to suspect that Kane could manage passage to Archepellan.

"I see. All right, I'll try. But it will cost you—Hysrac is quite ruthless when it comes to money."

There was a vidphone on the patio table; it was done quickly and without fuss. Kane winced at the fee: 5,000 credits—most of his remaining stake. In the end, it wouldn't matter about the money. If the Chirpones didn't pan out as suspects, he'd be out of time anyway.

After Beth had finished with Hysrac, Kane got up and walked over to her, offering his hands. She hesitated, then took them, and her skin was cool against his. He pulled her up and they kissed and a strange thing happened.

When he came to himself again, Elizabeth was sitting and crying softly; her dress was torn down the front, and someone held both of his arms behind him in an iron grip. Kane shook his head slowly to clear it, and the grip on his arms loosened.

"Elizabeth . . ."

She tried to say something, shook her head and pressed her hands against her face. Kane's muscles began to shake in reaction.

"You are all right now, Elias," Pendrake said with soft authority. Kane nodded and the alien released his arms.

"Beth, I'm sorry."

She looked up at him; gathered the front of her dress together.

"Perhaps your coat, Elias," Pendrake murmured. Kane slipped out of the V-coat, started to drape it around her shoulders and, when she stiffened, handed it to her instead. She tried to smile.

"It's all right. I know what it was. You've been . . . affected." She drew a shuddering breath and succeeded in a brittle smile before turning away. "Oh, Elias, what's going to become of us?"

He fought the urge to take her in his arms. "Are you going to be all right?"

"Yes, I'm . . . You didn't get very far with it before Pendrake . . . I'll be okay."

"Do you want me to leave?"

"No." She said it too quickly.

"I think it's best," he said after a moment, "that I not see you again until this is over."

"Get the Chirpones out of your system quickly, Elias, and find out what's happening to us."

"About the trip to Archepellan . . ."

"Be at pad fifteen in the restricted area at Kennedy early tomorrow morning. Someone will meet you. I . . . I'll not be there."

He nodded.

On the hopter flight back to the Alpha, Kane was silent. Pendrake said nothing but Kane was aware that the alien was watching him. He knew he should say something to ease Pendrake's concern, but lassitude gripped him. When they landed, he stirred and looked around at the nearby building tops for signs of Tulley's agents. There was no sign, other than the instincts sharpened during his days with Naval Intelligence, to tell him that the watchers were out there somewhere.

At 2:00 A.M. Kane gave up staring in the darkness at the ceiling and took a sleepdeep. In the few moments before unconsciousness it occurred to him that he felt no remorse for what he'd done to Beth that evening; only uneasiness over the missing emotion. His last thought was of something Tulley had said earlier that day: "I only know how I *should* feel. . . ."

At the six o'clock alarm, Kane took a ministim and trudged into Pendrake's room to wake the alien. The bed was neatly made; Pendrake was stretched out on the floor between his bed and the window. Kane nudged Pendrake's sole with his foot and the alien rolled to his feet as if he had not been asleep.

"Good morning, Elias."

"You must hate making beds."

"I prefer making them to sleeping on them," Pendrake said. He walked over to the mirror and smoothed his white hair backward, tying it in the customary bun at the back. Kane watched him, shaking his head.

"What would people say if they knew I had a valet who sleeps fully clothed?"

Pendrake smiled. "Unlike humans, we Cephantines are true sleepers. I lie down carefully, so as not to wrinkle my garments, and do not move at all during sleep. Since our bodies are cooled by gaseous rather than liquid exchange at the pores, and our skin does not require constant maintenance by body oils, I do not grow dirty as I sleep."

Kane could think of nothing to say and stalked off, muttering, to the shower. By the time he was clean and dressed in the gray skin suit Pendrake had laid out the night before, the alien had packed all their things. They breakfasted on rolls, Kane drinking the coffee that Pendrake spurned.

"Tulley can't spare many operatives to keep tabs on us," Kane said. "We'll make it tougher by splitting up. You leave first at ground level and walk down Madison Mall two blocks on one side and back three on the other. Then look up here and I'll blink my light-stick once if you're being followed and twice if you're not. If not, go straight to Kennedy via subway the way I told you last night and wait outside pad fifteen for me. If it's one blink, come on back and we'll try something else."

Pendrake nodded and slipped out. When he'd gone, Kane took their baggage up to the roof and hailed a hoptercab without looking around at the other roofs. The hopter came almost at once; he hoisted the luggage on board, climbed in and instructed the cab to take the bags to Kennedy Spaceport's main terminal roof and wait one hour for him to claim them. If he did not, the cab was to return to the Alpha roof and deposit the bags. He paid in advance and, just before the cab lifted off, rolled out the door and dropped to the roof, crouching in the shadow of the parapet and hoping Tulley's operative was not an amateur. After the hopter was well away from the roof, he stood and walked back to the drop shaft, checking covertly to make sure that the hopter had not been followed. They must think he had tried to lead them away—that the suitcases were empty props.

He returned quickly to his suite and looked down at the mall. At seven o'clock few people were around and he spotted the Cephantine almost immediately. He watched through a pair of binoculars as Pendrake made his circuits up and back. If someone was tailing him, they were either very good or they were too far back and would lose him as soon as he hit the subway. Kane flashed the light twice as the alien turned and looked up. Then he left for the lobby.

When he stepped out of the drop chute into the velvet and brass elegance of the lobby, he screened the room casually. There were three people besides the desk clerk—an old man in a webchair watching the New York *Times* on a lapfax, a maid who had just moved to the lobby entrance and was polishing the gleaming doors and a young man with dark glasses and a radeye strapped to his forehead. Kane rejected the blind man right away: Tulley was incapable of such subtlety. It was either the maid or the old man. Kane strolled over to the desk.

"Good morning, sir. May I help you?"

"You certainly may. Which one is the ImpSec agent?"

"I beg your pardon?" the clerk said without hesitation.

"Nothing. A little joke."

"I see." The man began to putter with some mail. Kane walked to the door feeling satisfied. The clerk had not shown that invariable hesitation which accompanies the unexpected. It followed that he had been informed of the ImpSec operative, as would have been necessary in the case of a new maid who suddenly showed up and began polishing the lobby.

The woman had taken up a good position, where he could not jam the door on his way out. He walked over; returned her smile. She was young and quite pretty and he did not doubt that she could crush his larynx or snap his collarbone with a single blow. He stabbed with two stiff fingers precisely below the sternum and eased her to the floor.

"Clerk! This woman has fainted—call a doctor."

"Here, you, sir, wait just a moment."

Kane stepped through the doors, pulled a length of plaswire from his pocket and bound the outside handles together with a looping motion. A bum across the mall looked up at him as he left the hotel, got up and began to shamble after him. Kane pretended not to notice, walking to the nearest subway entrance and cursing Tulley's thoroughness under his breath. As soon as he was out of sight on the subway stairway, he began to run, rounded the first curve and stopped long enough to hear the footsteps behind him.

When he reached the deserted platform, he slipped over the edge, crouching in the dirt by the tracks under the overhanging ledge. Footsteps echoed off the tiled mosaic across from him; he tried to still his breathing. The tracks a meter away began to vibrate and the odor of grease and oil, which had been in the background, snapped into focus. Above him a door slammed as the agent searched the rest rooms. A rumble swelled in the distance and light picked out blackened timbers in the tunnel and threw shadows which dimmed, then washed out. The brick trembled against his side and the roar of the train battered him. He pinched his eyes shut as grit stung his face and the train screeched to a stop at the platform and sat centimeters away, its heat and stench nearly stifling his breathing. Doors hissed open and shut, wheels slipped, then bit into the track, and the train pulled away. The tick of contracting metal from the rails signaled the return of Kane's hearing. He chinned himself slowly on the edge of the platform; it was empty.

The next train took him to the spaceport, where he claimed his bags and walked to the perimeter of pad fifteen. As he drew close to the departure gate he saw the squat bulk of a Chirpone cruiser distorted in heat shimmers from the pad. Pendrake was standing outside the gate, which was guarded by two Krythians.

Kane walked over to the Cephantine, and started to speak, when a hand fell on his shoulder and someone said, "Please keep your hands in sight, Mr. Kane. You are under arrest."

Chapter Seven

Kane held his arms away from his body and turned slowly. The man dropped his hand from Kane's shoulder and stepped back, keeping his stunner leveled. Kane sized him up quickly: fortyish, a pose of nonchalance and cynical half-lidded eyes. Perhaps he would deal.

"By whose authority am I under arrest?"

"Why, mine, of course. That is, until I call the commissioner. I'm sure he'll be happy to add his say once I tell him what you're up to."

"I am sorry, Elias. This man must have followed me."

"That's right, Mr. Kane. I'm afraid the gook, here, hasn't got your deviousness."

Kane made a decision about the man's fate. "What would you know about my deviousness?"

"Tut tut. You're here, aren't you? And I don't see my two colleagues."

"A hundred credits," Kane said.

"Two hundred, and your slave stays with me."

"Two, and Pendrake comes along. You wouldn't want him—he sleeps in his clothes."

The agent laughed. "Okay, but it's got to be cash. We can't have this sort of thing on record."

They went to the nearest terminal. Kane unloaded and pocketed the agent's stunner. The agent, in turn, threatened to stop departure of the Chirpone cruiser if Kane double-crossed him. Kane faxed the two hundred credits at an outlet and the agent counted the money. "Pleasure doing business with you," he said. "Of course, you realize that I'll have to tell Tulley that you left with the Chirpones, as soon as I think up a story about why I didn't stop you."

"Of course. Would you like me to give you a black eye? It would explain how I got away with your weapon."

The agent brightened. "Would you?"

"Elias, please." Pendrake looked sick.

"Why don't you go and get our luggage on the ship? I'll join you in a minute."

The two men went into a rest room; the agent pointed at the outer edge of his eye. "Not too hard, now."

Kane knocked him over the sink and into a mirror, which cracked under the blow. Then he took back the two hundred credits, dragged the body into a stall and walked to the ship, wondering if he should be feeling guilt.

Hysrac and his two bodyguards met him at the ship's portal. One of the Krythians handed him a translator device which molded itself comfortably to the inside of his ear.

"Gweetings, Mr. Kane, and welcome aboard my

vessel. I suggest you wetain the twanslator in your ear for the duwation of our twip and while you are on Archepellan. You will find it does not impede normal heawing. We have assigned you to unit twelve, which lies along the yellow path. Your servant is alweady stwapped in, and I suggest you join him as soon as you have, ah, completed the awwangement we agweed upon. We plan to depart in ten minutes."

Kane nodded and signed the 5,000 credits over to Hysrac. There were a number of different-colored lines along the floor at his feet. Following the yellow one, he found his way through a labyrinth of corridors to the unit marked with both alien script and a number twelve. The door slid open as he reached for the handle. Pendrake lay enmeshed in a web of semiresilient straps which hung from the ceiling like a net hammock. The hammock bobbed when the alien tried to swing around at Kane's entrance.

"You look like a trussed pig."

"Your own wit may soon elude you," Pendrake said a bit sourly.

Kane climbed, smiling, into the other hammock and inspected the room. It was shaped like a squat cone and the walls were featureless except for a port, which was closed.

"An odd shape," Kane said.

"Hysrac said it helps dissipate acceleration forces."

"Not much furniture, either."

"The walls conceal a number of things—chairs, an eating table and an autocaf. The lines of the cabinets are difficult to see because of the high luminosity, but one of Hysrac's mute companions showed me how everything works. Incidentally, you will note that the

Chirpones follow the civilized custom of sleeping on the floor."

Kane grunted.

"Some of the units are much bigger than this one," Pendrake went on. "I passed one on the way in that I believe was being readied for an Argellian hermaphrodite."

"Those huge six-legged elephant creatures?"

"That is right. My people and theirs have enjoyed a cultural exchange treaty for over three thousand of your years. They are very amiable beings."

The door cycled open again and Hysrac entered with his two Krythians. The bodyguards lifted more straps from the floor and secured them to the bottoms of the two hammocks.

"I apologize for the delay," Hysrac said, "but it seems there is considewable pwessure fwom the ImpSec Buweau to delay our departure and come aboard our vessel."

Kane groaned; he'd hit the man hard enough to keep him out for an hour. Someone must have found him and revived him. "Are you going to let them in?"

"Much as it tewwifies me to wefuse, it is quite out of the question, as I have explained to them wepeatedly. Our optimum window on Archepellan will pass within fifteen minutes, after which much gweater fuel expenditure would be wequired. There is a commissioner—Clayton Tulley. He says he is a fwiend of yours and wishes to talk with you before you depart. I have bwought you a weceiver, but I implore you to be bwief. We must depart vewy soon."

"I'll not delay you."

"Good. We'll wait in the cowwidor; call us when you're thwough, and we'll wemove the weceiver."

Tulley's face was congested with blood and he cut off Kane's greeting.

"You've ripped it this time, Kane. You'll rot in a cell if you ever set foot on Earth again. You've thumbed your nose at me and the bureau and run off under the wings of an alien government."

"Clay, you've got to trust me. There are reasons—when I get back I'll brief you."

Tulley started to say something and Kane punched the cutoff; signaled for the Krythians to remove the receiver. A few minutes after they had gone, the ship began to float upward, lifted through Earth's gravity well by the antigravs. When the ship reached the outer fringe of the atmosphere, the main drives cut in, slamming them against the webbing. Acceleration continued until Kane's back ached and breathing became an effort. Finally the pressure dropped; Kane extricated himself from the sling and set out to explore the ship. The journey to Archepellan would last eight days, including jumps, but his best chance to look around should be now, while the crew was still busy securing from liftoff.

For a while he wandered through the corridors of the passenger section, meeting no one; then he descended to the cargo holds where he found his way barred by a Krythian. The creature did not bother to draw his weapon but stood in Kane's way. When Kane tried to step around him, the Krythian's eyestalks swiveled and the alien cut him off.

"Just exploring, pal. Is there something down here you don't want me to see?"

"Of course there isn't," said a voice behind him. Kane turned in surprise. Hysrac, flanked by the ever-present bodyguards, regarded him with what might have been amusement. "Feel perfectly fwee to look awound all you choose," said the Chirpone, waving the guard in the passage to one side. "In fact, I was just looking for you with the intention of giving you a tour."

"How thoughtful. You needn't trouble yourself—I can just stroll around . . ."

"It's no twouble. This journey is long for me too. Besides, I'm wather pwoud of our wares and it would give me considewable pleasure to show them off. Of course, much of my owiginal inventowy has been sold on the planet wun which I have just concluded on Tewwa." Hysrac led him past holds stacked with the remnants of fragrant Roolean spice lots, bolts of Kad-axed mood cloth—currently the fashion rage on Earth—Argellian wines and brandies and a few left-over Shul-Rubid devices. The bottom-most hold was larger than the rest and contained five or six potted musal trees, all in the fruit-bearing phase.

"I suppose this is your snack supply for the trip," Kane said, drawing in the fragrance of the humid soil mixed with the tang of the fruit globes.

"You jest, but you are cowwect."

"Seems inefficient, taking along the whole tree. Why not just crate up the fruit?"

"We would pwefer that, of course, but it is quite impossible. The fwuit spoils vewy fast once it is picked and we have not yet discovered a pweservative which does not likewise wuin the taste."

Kane nodded. "Thanks for the tour."

"My pleasure, Mr. Kane. Is there anything else you'd like to see?"

"No," Kane lied.

"Then perhaps you would like to join some of the other passengers in the lounge."

There were two colonists and a Terran diplomat in the round, padded lounge, along with a Brull architect and three Moitan fish people in their potassium water tanks. Kane played poker with the humans for the next five hours, pausing only to eat yeasteaks and coffee from the autocaf and to watch the early stage of transition to paradoxical space. By the time they were in midtrans and the rich swirl of colors outside the ports had begun to pale, Kane had carefully won a small stake, mostly at the expense of the uncaring diplomat.

Despite his winnings he found himself growing more and more withdrawn as the game progressed. Near the end it occurred to him that he was not enjoying himself, a realization that depressed him even further. The game of poker, at the stakes for which he was playing, had never failed to amuse him before. The failure of that pleasure now gave him a feeling of loss. It seemed impossible that only days earlier he had stood in the elegance of the casino and worried that his passion for gambling had become a sick compulsion. Now, in a lull within another game whose ultimate stakes were his life and the lives of everyone on Earth, he could find no excitement in his most treasured vice. That he should want that excitement now was absurd, and no less true for all of its absurdity. He pushed back from the table, said his good nights and followed the yellow line back to his unit.

When the door slid open, he first noticed that the lights were out, then that Pendrake was lying in an odd position on the floor, and finally that something like plaswire glinted around the alien's wrists and ankles. Then it seemed he could feel each millimeter of depression of the back of his skull, each discrete point on the rising curve of pain, each degree of arc through which he fell, until blackness blotted out the impact of his face against the floor.

Chapter Eight

Hearing, as always, returned first. Kane listened to the low hum and struggled back to awareness. He seemed to be lying on his stomach with his hands beneath him. He tried to wiggle his fingers and the needles of fading circulation brought him to full consciousness. Something rolled against his leg and he realized that he was being moved around a curve. The hum resolved itself into the murmur of a gravsled. He opened one eye and Pendrake's head and shoulders edged into focus about ten centimeters away. Bubbles of saliva formed on the alien's lips with each exhalation. Kane tried to move his fingers again but this time they felt dead; his feet had not been tied, though.

The sled rounded another corner and stopped. Kane squinted out of the corner of one eye, ignoring the pain which knifed his head, and tried to get a fix on where he was. Something whirred and clicked and red light mingled with the illumination of the corridor; Kane realized where they were—a hull air lock. He rolled off the gravsled and stumbled to his feet, his knotted hands out front. The man who'd been pulling the sled whirled and Kane got a quick impression—pinched eyes, a mouth surrounded by small white scars. He was not one of the people from the lounge who were supposed to comprise the entire human complement of the ship.

The man whipped a dowel about half a meter long from his belt and rushed to Kane. The club scythed air and the man's momentum carried him forward. Kane's kick landed above the knee, but still snapped the man's leg stiff, drawing a grunt as the cartilage stretched. Kane held his hands out front and placed his feet wider than his shoulders, pivoting as the man circled him more warily. The red light lent the scene a garish look, as though they were performing at a circus side show, but the room was quiet except for their harsh breathing.

The man snarled and waded in, swinging the club back and forth in front. Kane took a few blows on the hands, feeling nothing, then kicked the man's hip, driving him against a wall. He followed up while the man was off balance, rotating his own body on one leg so that the other could snap at the wrist that held the club. Bone cracked and the man gasped as his club clattered to the floor. He recovered; drew a short knife with his left hand. Pain began to squeeze Kane's head; his vision blurred. He lifted his right toe in a feint aimed at the man's gut, flipped his body over on one leg and rammed the heel upward, connecting with the jaw even as the blade raked his thigh. The thrust of the blow carried him into the man, they fell together in a tangle and Kane knew it was over—one way or the other. The knife did not plunge into Kane's exposed back; he rolled off the man and was sick on the floor.

"A-h-h-h-hk." The noise came from the gravsled. Kane wiped his mouth with purple-gray hands; watched Pendrake roll over and sit up.

"Elias, you are ill."

"Poleaxed, wrapped in plaswire and slashed," Kane corrected.

"Your hands!" Pendrake snapped the wire on his own wrists and ankles as though it were thread and bounded to Kane's side. In seconds he had Kane's bonds off too and was chafing life back into the hands. "I believe no permanent damage has occurred," he said after a moment. "It is a pity your flesh and veins are so yielding."

"Ar-r-rg," Kane said as fire began to dance along his fingers. "I think my thumb's broken."

Pendrake shuddered. "You people are so barbaric."

Kane noticed several welts on the side of the alien's skull. "Looks like he nailed you pretty good, too."

"Four times, I believe."

"You counted?"

"It may have been five—I probably would not remember the last one."

"And you just stood there."

"The man was blocking my way to the door; I could not move him aside without injuring him." Pendrake tore a strip from his tunic and bound up the knife wound in Kane's leg. "Fortunately, he missed your major blood vessels and connective tissue," the alien murmured. "I am no expert on human anatomy, but I predict you will suffer only pain from this wound."

"What else is there?" Kane said with a groan.

The man Kane had felled rolled over, shaking his head drunkenly. Kane snatched the knife from the floor and brought the point of it under the man's chin.

"Elias . . ."

"I'm all right, Pendrake; I swear it."

The man groaned and opened his eyes. "Wha . . .?"

"Who are you?" Kane demanded.

The man glared at him. Pendrake moved close to Kane and grasped his elbow out of sight of the man. Kane knew if he tried to stab upward, the alien's grip would stop him. He pressed the blade as hard as he dared against the man's neck. "Speak up."

"Anders. Cole Anders," the man growled.

"Why did you try to kill us?"

"Ye be after the gentle ones. Ye will hound them to death with thy madness."

Kane glanced at Pendrake; the man was a colonist—an accent that thick would be difficult to fake. "Who are *they*?"

"The Chuh-Chirpones." His face twisted. Kane eased the pressure of the knife but the man's grimace only intensified. "They be innocent," he gasped. "No Earthie scum be going to hurt them."

"Did they put you up to this?"

"Gods, no!" The man's eyes widened in denial. "Ye could not say it if ye knew them."

"Who, then?"

"I act for . . . no other man." Anders' head fell to the side and he sighed. Kane dropped the knife and let the body slide away from him.

"I will see if there is a medivac on board," Pendrake said.

"He's dead."

"Dead? But how?" Pendrake's face lengthened in shock. He bent over the man, pressed an ear to his chest. After a moment he rocked back on his heels. "This is a terrible thing, Elias."

"Awful. All he did was try and shove us out an air lock."

"The fight—did you strike a killing blow?"

"I don't think so. I've been in one or two scrapes and I know what it takes to kill a man. The only really good blow I landed was to his chin. That could have snapped his neck on the spot or broken his jaw, but it didn't. It could be a slow cerebral hemorrhage or it could be something else."

"Something else?"

"A preconditioned heart stoppage."

"Do you mean," Pendrake said slowly, "that this man's heart could be made to stop in response to some conditioned stimulus?"

"Something in my questioning, probably. It gets done; the technique requires considerable skill and subtlety—especially if the victim has not agreed to the procedure and is unaware of it."

"Who would give his consent for such a thing?"

"People in the intelligence business mostly. The point can come where death is a mercy. . . ." Kane fell silent at the look on Pendrake's face. "Anyway, we'll need an autopsy to be sure."

The inner lock spun and the door clanged open to admit two Krythians, blasters drawn. They leveled their weapons at Kane and Pendrake and waited while a Chirpone even shorter and more plump than

Hysrac stepped over the low sill and surveyed the scene. When he saw the dead man, the Chirpone shrank back against the wall.

"What is going on here?" he piped.

"Who are you?" Kane said. The two Krythians stiffened but the Chirpone gestured and they remained still.

"Forgive me. I am Hasys, captain of this vessel. And you are, I pwesume, Mr. Kane and his servant, Pendwake. What are you doing in this air lock? What has happened to the other human?"

In terse language Kane sketched out the events since he'd returned to his unit that evening.

Hasys shuddered. "Awful. Awful. There will be a full investigation, of course."

"Do you know the identity of this man?" Kane asked.

The Chirpone edged toward the body and peered at the face. "Why, it's Major Anders, I believe."

"*Major* Anders?"

"He was one of the owiginal party of colonists who cwashlanded on Archepellan and made the first contact between your species and ours."

"I thought I had met all the other humans on board. Why did none of us know about this man?"

"My dear fellow, no attempt was made on our part to keep such information fwom you, believe me. Perhaps Major Anders merely wished to be undisturbed. He has been a passenger on our ships to Earth sevewal times, and has never appeared overly sociable with others of his wace."

"Why is that?"

"Please, Mr. Kane. I am not a human psychologist."

Kane considered. "Where does he board your ships when he comes to Earth?"

"Why, Archepellan, of course. Major Anders wetired fwom the Centauwan Navy shortly after his ship cwash-landed on our planet. I believe he has since become a natuwalized quasi-citizen of Archepellan."

Kane nodded. Was it possible that the man had become such a zealot for the Chirpones that he would kill to prevent them from being harassed? Kane remembered Elizabeth Tyson's almost fanatical devotion to the alien traders. There was another factor, too. Cole Anders *was* a colonist. "I'll want an autopsy," Kane muttered half to himself.

Hasys thumbed his bill-like mouth and hesitated. "I do not doubt that an autopsy will be wanted, Mr. Kane, but I fear you are hardly the one to demand it." The alien edged backward out the door and Kane noticed that the Krythians had kept their blasters aimed at his chest throughout the conversation.

"What do you mean?"

"Fwom this moment, you are to consider yourself under awwest," the Chirpone said, "on suspicion of murder."

Chapter Nine

Kane stood in the corridor and listened for any sound. The Krythians had stopped following him after his protest to Hysrac, but they might still be hanging around just out of sight. He'd deliberately waited until the eighth and final day of their journey to Archepellan, allowing the furor over Major Anders' death to die down a bit. The two colonists were now avoiding him, and the diplomat, while civil, was happy to leave him alone. That left the Krythians and the Chirpones. Hysrac had called the arrest a mere formality, to be dispensed with by joint attention of the Terran Embassy and the Chirpone Government as soon as the ship landed. Kane reserved judgment.

Now, satisfied that he was alone, he hurried through the corridors to the forward sections of the ship. The Chirpone vessel was laid out somewhat like Earth ships; the corridor he was following narrowed and he encountered several dead ends before finding the one remaining passage that pushed forward into the nose of the ship. At the end of the passage there was a bulkhead door. Kane noticed that it was twice as tall as the Chirpones he'd seen. There was a conventional handle on the lock door; Kane was reaching out for it when the voice stopped him.

"Mr. Kane, what bwings you to this part of the ship?"

Kane turned in surprise. "Hysrac. I didn't hear you come up . . ." Kane trailed off as he realized that the alien was alone—the two usual Krythians were not with him. It was the first time he'd seen a Chirpone without bodyguards. "Where are your friends? Aren't you afraid that I'll jump you or something?"

"More afwaid than you can possibly imagine," Hysrac replied. "I did not expect to see you here—I was coming forward to get an ETA fwom Captain Hasys and I didn't feel a bodyguard would be necessary since this is not the passenger section of the ship. I implore you to make no moves of any kind in my diwection."

Feet pounded in the corridor and Hysrac's bodyguards ran up to his side, their blasters drawn.

"Don't they know how to do anything but point those things," Kane complained.

"They have other talents, I assure you." Hysrac did not instruct the Krythians to holster their weapons. "Is there something that has pwompted you to investigate this part of the vessel?" he asked again.

Kane pointed at the bulkhead. "Is that the bridge?"

"Yes, but I'm afwaid you will find the door securely locked."

"Why is that?"

"I should think the answer would be obvious. Your pwoximity cweates considewable stwess among my wace. Piloting a space vessel is a demanding pwocedure—we could not permit it to be diswupted by your pwesence, however bwief and kindly intentioned."

"Of course. Forgive my thoughtlessness. Perhaps you would have no objection if I looked over the bridge after we've landed and the crew has departed—I'm an old navy dog and spaceships fascinate me."

Hysrac hesitated. "I'm afwaid I could not permit that either, Mr. Kane. You humans give off the chawactewistic odor of the hunting and killing animal. This ship will be departing again as soon as it can be loaded with new goods. Your lingewing smell on the bwidge could be a source of distwess and distwaction to the cwew."

Kane had to work to follow Hysrac's explanation, as a thought distracted him. He'd had the thought several times: *why did the translator device in his ear handle every nuance of phonology except for the r's?* Hysrac seemed to be awaiting his reaction; he forced himself to consider the alien's objection and wondered why it rang so false. Why would Hysrac lie to prevent him from seeing the bridge?

"I see," he said simply.

"If you would like to study the bwidge of one of our vessels at your leisure, I suggest you visit your Smithsonian Institution on Tewwa. We have donated an exact weplica to that museum for all to see."

"Yes, of course. I'll do that."

"And now I suggest you weturn to your unit and pwepare for decelewation. I'm sure we'll be landing soon. Kaaman will accompany you and help you stwap in."

After the Krythian had adjusted Kane's and Pendrake's floor straps and left, Kane fumbled with his webbing and clambered down.

"Elias, what are you doing?"

Kane pulled out a suitcase and popped open the hidden recess. "I've got an errand to run," he said, "and this is the best time to do it." He took out a sliver of plaswire with a pinhead-sized broadcaster on one end.

"We are going to suffer multi-G deceleration forces at any moment; you could be severely injured if you are not in your webbing."

"That's what makes this the best time. No one else will be in the corridors."

Pendrake craned his neck to see the compartment in Kane's suitcase. "First that ugly weapon and now this strange device. Suitcases with false bottoms hardly seem the usual equipment of an unemployed scholar."

"I had a friend in naval intelligence," Kane said. "We used to play cloak and dagger games and he shared some of his equipment with me. I told you; I'm interested in everything."

"Stand by for multi-G conditions," said a voice from the walls.

"Elias . . ."

"Got to go. See you in a bit." Kane ran into the hallway and sprinted through the deserted corridors toward the nose of the ship. Warning lights flashed on the walls; he ignored the clamor of his nerves and the sweat which soaked his suit and ran to the bulkhead door at which Hysrac had surprised him only moments before. He smoothed the plaswire over the seam of the door on the hinge side and gave the tiny broadcaster a half twist. He was most of the way back to his unit when the corridor tipped and became a well. He fell about three feet, smashing against one of the bulkhead walls which vertically ringed the corridor at regular intervals. As he fell, he brought his knees up to cushion his chest. Pain shot through his legs and his head rang from slamming into the bulkhead, but somehow he remained conscious. Only a few feet away, the units on the other side of the corridor walls turned on their axes, aligning their floors with the stern of the ship as it hurtled bottom-down into Archepellan's gravity well. Kane sucked air and tried to untwist his neck, but the G-forces pinned him securely. Then deceleration eased abruptly and the ship resumed its former orientation. Kane slid down the bulkhead wall and began to crawl. After a moment he was able to stand and stagger the remaining distance to his and Pendrake's unit. The door opened and he fell against the alien.

"My suitcase!" It came out a hoarse whisper. "The brown vial—get me a capsule."

Pendrake eased him to the floor and brought the megastim and a squeeze tube of water. Kane popped the capsule and swallowed, waiting with bowed head while the stimulant flooded his system. Pendrake took the squeeze tube and a cloth and wiped the clotting blood from Kane's upper lip and chin.

"Stop fussing. I'll be all right." Kane glanced expectantly at the door; the megastim surged through him and he felt strong and alert. Within five hours, he knew, his body would begin paying. He walked over to the port and studied the glistening silver-blue horizon of Archepellan, which curved slightly in the near distance. It looked much as Earth might from a few hundred kilometers in space; they should set down within the hour. The door slid open behind him.

"Mr. Kane, you weathered decelewation without difficulty?"

"Why shouldn't I?" He swung around and faced Captain Hasys. The alien looked him over in slow appraisal.

"Indeed you should have had no problem—our anti-G slings are quite adequately designed if one is pwoperly seated. I was merely inquiwing as a courtesy."

"Very gracious of you," Kane said dryly. "What happens when we land?"

"Hyswac has awwanged for you to simply accompany an escort to the Tewwan Embassy. Your Ambassador Bwace and our Pwefect Eswyhon will conduct a joint inquiwy to determine what action, if any, should be taken."

"What about Anders' autopsy?"

"I pwesume that will be performed by the embassy physician, a Dr. Gween. If you wish to be pwesent, you should contact him." The captain turned to leave.

"Just a minute."

"Yes, Mr. Kane?"

"You don't approve of me, do you?"

"I neither appwove nor disappwove. You are what you are."

There it was again; that maddening Chirpone fatalism. "But you actually believe I murdered your Major Anders?"

"That is a matter for the inquiwy."

"Would it upset you if I did kill him?"

"My dear Mr. Kane, what is the point of all this? What diffewence does it make if I am upset or not? The man is dead."

"Yes." Kane studied the alien. If Hasys felt any grief at Cole Anders' death, he was concealing it well. And yet the major had seemed so devoted to the Chirpones.

"Is there anything else?"

"One other thing. If you would not object, I'd like to meet your crew—after they've disembarked, of course. I'd like to thank them for a comfortable and well-navigated journey."

"That's weally unnecessawy, though you are kind to think of it . . ."

"I wouldn't detain them, I'd stay well away. Just a few words?"

Hasys appeared to consider. "Vewy well. Wait at the side of the landing pad and I'll intwoduce my officers as soon as they've completed shutdown."

After the captain and his Krythian escort had left, Kane took a device resembling a wrist watch out of his suitcase and carefully set the hands as Pendrake watched.

"Your behavior is quite mysterious," the alien complained.

"I'll explain after we're off the ship." Kane returned his gaze to the port. They were well within the pull of Archepellan's gravity now and their velocity had dropped enough to permit the antigravs to engage; the ship descended toward the planet as gently as a drifting balloon. In a short time they broke through the high cloud cover and Kane caught his first glimpse of the alien planet. He was not prepared for what he saw.

"It's mostly forest," he said. "Trees everywhere, as far as you can see. They must be bringing us down on some backwater."

"I understood we were to land at the planetary capital," Pendrake replied. "A place called Ixyon."

Kane shook his head. "It's hardly a town. There's a lot of pad area and a little cluster of buildings around a square . . ." He fell to musing as the cruiser descended. Could this be the capital of a race of aliens powerful or ambitious enough to embark on the conquest of Earth, even by a nonfrontal strategy? What would they have to gain? He could see spots of violet and yellow through the spreading treetops, which stretched to the horizon in all directions around the spaceport. Sunlight glinted off the small armada of space vessels—none larger than cruiser class—and sparkled on the jade-colored towers of the nearby town. The ship settled and within minutes they had stepped down the telescoping ramp into a moist, oxygen-rich atmosphere. The temperature was mild and a gentle breeze stirred the waist-high orange grass around the perimeter of the field. As they stood at the foot of the ship, a metallic-gray ground car slid to a stop nearby and a tall man wearing the dress reds of the Federated Terran Marine Corps stepped down and walked briskly toward them.

"Mr. Kane?" he inquired.

"Lieutenant Elias Kane, retired."

"Yes, sir. I'm to accompany you and your servant to the embassy."

"One moment, Sergeant." Kane watched as Hasys led a contingent of Chirpones and five Krythians down the exit ramp and across the pad toward him. He checked the watch-device on his arm and a hollow feeling began in his stomach.

"Mr. Kane, may I intwoduce my cwew."

Kane nodded as Hasys made the introductions, then mumbled some mechanical words of thanks. The sergeant stood on one foot then the other until Kane had finished, then stepped forward and took his arm. "Would you like to come along now—sir?"

Without seeming to, Kane slid his arm free. "No, I don't think so."

"But my orders . . ."

"Is this Federation territory, Sergeant?"

"No, but . . ."

"Then you have no authority here, do you?"

"I'm not an interplanetary lawyer. I have my orders. You should understand that—Lieutenant."

"Oh, I do understand that. That's why I'm not coming with you. Tell your C.O. to inform Ambassador Brace that I'll get in touch with him soon about the death of Major Anders and certain other matters. Tell him not to conduct the autopsy until I've gotten in touch with him."

Hasys, who had been listening intently to the exchange, stepped forward. "Mr. Kane, do I understand that you wefuse to co-opewate with your own authowities?"

"Do you intend to take action if I don't?"

Hasys hesitated. "Unilatewal action will no doubt be taken by my government if you will not put yourself under the juwisdiction of your own. After all, Major Anders was a quasi-citizen of Archepellan. But surely you see what an awkward position you put us in. . . ."

"I think I'll take my chances with you fellows for now," Kane said. "Is there a place in Ixyon—not part of embassy territory, mind you—where Pendrake and I can be accommodated?"

"The Inn of Stones caters to alien guests fwom all over the galaxy, but . . ."

"Then your government can contact me there at their convenience." Pendrake had gotten their luggage from a gravsled and now stood next to the sergeant, a resigned expression on his face.

"If you're counting on the peaceful Chirpones to let you escape justice," the sergeant said, "you should know that the Krythians handle the messy police work here. They aren't shy about it either."

"I'm sure they're not."

"And you still won't come with me?"

Kane shook his head and Pendrake sighed audibly.

"Okay. At least I can offer you a ride into town."

Kane glanced at the nearby towers of Ixyon. "Thanks for your offer, but I think we'd reach town faster on foot."

The marine glared at him and put a hand on the butt of his blaster, but let it drop when Hasys backed off gibbering and the Krythians stepped forward fingering their weapons.

"I'll be seeing you again, *Mister* Kane." He turned and stalked back to the waiting ground car. Hasys snapped an order, and the Chirpones and all but one of the Krythians moved off toward a building at the edge of the spaceport. The remaining Krythian stayed at a distance, watching Kane and Pendrake.

"The sergeant may cause trouble," Pendrake murmured.

Kane shrugged. "I can't risk being bundled back to

Earth and the good commissioner on some trumped-up charge just yet. Things are beginning to get interesting."

"What do you mean?"

"What did you think of Hasys' crew?"

Pendrake looked mystified. "I saw nothing unusual about them."

"I didn't either," Kane said slowly, "except that they are *not* Hasys' crew. Not unless they somehow managed to get off the cruiser without opening the only door to the ship's bridge."

Chapter Ten

Kane peeked into the hall and smiled at the Krythian outside before easing the door shut again and turning to examine his room. The room looked primitive, with walls of the same rough green substance as composed the outside of the building—a material softer than jade and with a slightly higher reflectance. One wall had been chiseled into a crude bas-relief of rolling hills, through which wandered a river bordered by low trees. A square of light fell through the room's single open window onto the bed—a large four-poster with a frame of burnished blue metal. There were no other furnishings except a rough cloth curtain at one side of the window; Pendrake's room, on the next level down, was even more austere, lacking a bed. As Kane watched, a breeze stirred the edge of the curtain and carried in the spicy fragrance of musal from the courtyard outside.

"The Krythian is still in the hall?" Pendrake asked.

Kane nodded. "He'll be there until the Chirpones decide on their next move."

"Why do you think Hasys tried to deceive you about the crew?"

"I don't know, but it's the first proof we've had that the Chirpones might not be what they seem."

"Perhaps the captain merely did not wish to risk your upsetting his real crew, so he arranged for the masquerade."

"Maybe." Kane consulted his watch for the tenth time that hour; saw that the hands were moving normally. "But you'll have to explain to me why the door to the bridge still hasn't opened. When and if it does, both hands on this watch will move to twelve o'clock and stay there."

"Could your transmitter be defective?"

"Not likely."

"What is your theory, then?"

"I've got three of them. One, the ship may be fully automatic, though I know of no technology in the universe which would make it possible. Two, the ship may be piloted by some species other than the Chirpones. One reason I originally wanted a peek at the bridge was to see whether they're really capable of running a ship in deep space. If they are, it would seem inconsistent with their cowardly instincts—one paradoxical jump miscalculation and you can land in a sun. If we assume that they've hired another species to do their piloting for them—perhaps a non-oxygen-breathing race requiring a special environment on a sealed bridge—then we could understand why the crew might still be on the bridge."

"Except that one might then wonder why the Chirpones wish to conceal such an alliance," Pendrake pointed out. "What is your third hypothesis?"

"Has it occurred to you to wonder about the Chirpones' retainers?"

"The Krythians? But they are so servile one would never suspect them."

"Exactly. Haven't you wondered how the Chirpones can tolerate hired muscle from another planet—especially since they profess to accept no guarantees about behavior. How do they know their paid mercenaries won't turn on them? Why don't they go around in a state of perpetual panic?"

"It is an intriguing suspicion, Elias, but as a nonhuman, perhaps I can offer another perspective."

"I'm listening."

"I was not present when you talked with Hysrac, but your description of that encounter made much more sense to me than it did to you. As I recall, you and Hysrac disagreed on a fundamental point. He believes that behavior is determined and controlled by environment. You believe, as do nearly all humans, that you behave according to your intentions."

"Wait a minute. I accept that the environment helps to shape my thoughts and intentions."

"Yes, but you believe that, in the end, your mind is what controls your actions."

"We went through all that," Kane said. "Hysrac seems to believe that thinking is just another form of behavior. To him, thoughts may go along with behaviors but if you think your thoughts are controlling your behaviors, you're fooling yourself. But what's this got to do with the Krythians?"

"Simply this. You humans are the only race I have encountered that believes its behavior is controlled and determined from within rather than by events and forces outside you."

"So?"

"Suppose Hysrac is right and you are wrong."

"It shouldn't make any difference. My behavior would still be the same."

"Pardon me, Elias, but I do not think so."

"Now you're contradicting yourself. Either my thoughts make a difference or they don't. If Hysrac is right, and my intentions don't control my behavior, then he should have less to fear from me, not more—one less unknown to worry about."

"It is more complex than that," Pendrake said. "Hysrac never claimed that your thoughts have no effect on your behavior; only that they do not *control* your behavior as most humans believe. The distinction is difficult; suppose you were pointing a blaster at me and you believed that it contained no charge—that it was harmless. Suppose, further, that I knew of your belief and also knew that the blaster was in fact fully charged. What would be my attitude toward you?"

"Fear. Mistrust."

"Precisely. The blaster is loaded whether you *perceive* it to be or not—there is only one external reality, but there exist two internal realities—your belief and mine. The result could be fatal for me because your behavior is no longer predictable from the external reality."

"You're saying Hysrac is afraid of me because I am unpredictable and that I am unpredictable because I misperceive and misinterpret reality—that it's not my thoughts that control my behavior but my perceptions of reality."

"Perceptions that Hysrac regards as erroneous," Pendrake said, nodding. "Regardless of who is right about what controls behavior, the fact remains that the human race is an exception to the galactic rule—a group of beings whose behavior, including its thoughts, appears insane to the galactic community. This was true even before the psychopath plague, and is doubly true now. Because of this, the Chirpones may fear you and yet trust the Krythians, who follow the rules of rationality as they are jointly perceived by both cultures. This does not mean that neither race is capable of violence, even against each other, merely that both operate by the same rule of circumstance imposed from without. The Chirpones' fear of humanity, like most fears, is rooted in uncertainty."

Kane walked to the window and leaned on the sill, surveying the courtyard below. It was empty except for a single Krythian who stood under a musal tree looking up at him. The alien had not been there earlier. "You're saying that all of Hysrac's talk about cowardice might really be a polite euphemism for a more specific fear—a fear of the human race?"

"It is difficult to see yourself through the eyes of the galaxy," the alien said. "Even so, I have found much to admire in your species, despite its unpredictable savagery."

Kane turned and smiled ironically. "Then you are not frightened of me?"

"I have never been frightened of anything or anyone," the alien said matter-of-factly. "Fear is as foreign to the nature of a Cephantine as it is instinctive to the Chirpones."

"As it *appears* instinctive," Kane corrected.

Pendrake nodded.

"I'm glad one of us is never afraid," Kane said, looking toward the door, "because I think the Krythians are moving in on us."

As if this remark were a summons, the door swung inward and two Krythians dressed in glittering mail stalked into the room. One of them handed Kane a pale green card.

" 'Your immediate presence is invited by the Honorable Esryhon, Prefect of Police,' " Kane read. He looked at the Krythians. "And if I refuse?" The aliens stared at him in apparent lack of comprehension. Kane walked over to the bed and sat down; the Krythians drew their blasters and he stood again, quickly. "Just checking."

They walked out of the Inn of Stones and down a shaded avenue made from cobbled pieces of the green rock. A few Chirpones in colorful dress, each with a Krythian in attendance, passed by on the far side of the avenue before the Krythians led Kane and Pendrake into a cool narrow alley. Kane strained his eyes in the near darkness; up ahead water gurgled and a square of light grew until they stepped into a sunlit garden arranged around a fountain. To one side, at a low table, sat the tallest and thinnest Chirpone Kane had yet seen. He was guarded by the usual two Krythians.

"Please be seated; thank you for joining me."

"Did we have a choice?"

"Certainly, though I doubt you would have pweferred the alternative. But we are a civilized people, Mr. Kane; it disturbs me to talk of such things. Let us dispense with this unpleasant inquiwy into the death of Major Anders. You understand, your embassy still wishes to question you on its own; however, since you have wefused to put yourself into their juwisdiction, we have no alternative but to pwoceed alone."

Kane nodded.

"Vewy well. I have listened to the deposition of Captain Hasys and I must say that the circumstances of Major Anders' death are quite peculiar. I understand that both of you bore signs of a stwuggle?"

Kane's leg began to throb where the knife had struck. "The wounds of both of us were minor," he said. "In my opinion, Anders' wounds were also minor—certainly insufficient to cause death."

"The autopsy would appear to support that view."

Kane sat forward. "You mean it's been done already? What were the results?"

"Dr. Gween, the embassy physician, says that Major Anders died of massive heart failure, pwobably bwought on by the exertion of the fight."

Kane settled back. Heart failure, brought on by exertion—or by a preconditioned heart stoppage. "Then I don't see why this inquiry is necessary. It's clear I didn't kill him."

"Even so, we must satisfy ourselves on the extent of your culpability. You claim that Major Anders assaulted first your servant and then you, and that he was in the pwocess of pushing you out the air lock when you awoke and stopped him."

"That's right."

Esryhon turned to Pendrake. "Can you vewify this?"

"Unfortunately I was unconscious through much of what happened. I only awoke after the fight had ended."

"I see. A pity."

"However," Pendrake continued, "Major Anders definitely was the one who attacked me and knocked me senseless. Furthermore, when I regained consciousness, Major Anders was alive and, more importantly, Mr. Kane's hands were tightly bound. I am satisfied that he would not and indeed could not have bound them himself; this fact alone exculpates him in my mind."

"And in mine as well; I accept your explanation, of course. Mr. Kane, I see no weason to detain you further."

"Just like that?"

Esryhon stroked his mouth. "The word of a Cephantine is wespected thwoughout the galaxy, Mr. Kane, except, it appears, on Tewwa. Our only intewest fwom the beginning has been justice. In fact, it now appears that we owe you an apology. Major Anders was a quasi-citizen of Archepellan; as a wepwesentative of our government, allow me to expwess my wegwet at his attack on you and your servant. I twust that the west of your stay with us will be pleasant."

Kane read the dismissal. "Just one thing before we leave."

"Certainly."

"The autopsy—were there any other abnormalities besides those associated with heart failure?"

"The weport states that Major Anders was completely normal in all other wespects—except, of course, for the wounds you inflicted. If you wish more details, you should consult Dr. Gween." Esryhon stood; Kane and Pendrake followed suit. "Enjoy your stay. Oh yes—I should warn you—do not stway too far into the fowest without a Kwythian guide."

"May I ask why?"

"Out planet is a pawadise, Mr. Kane, and like all pawadises it contains a serpent."

Kane felt surprise at the prefect's apparent reference to ancient Terran lore.

"Archepellan's serpent is a formidable beast," Esryhon continued, "but you need not fear it so long as you stay in the city. Good day."

The Krythian that had followed them since they left the ship was nowhere to be seen as they walked back to the inn.

"That was quite painless, was it not?" Pendrake said as they stepped from the alley back into the street.

"So is an anesthetic," Kane replied. "I have the feeling that they're leaving the rough stuff to others."

"The embassy?"

"It would be far better for the Chirpones if my own people dealt with us."

"What can we do?"

"Suit yourself. I've got a megastim to sleep off."

Pendrake grunted. "And after that?"

"Why, we'll break into the Chirpone cruiser, of course."

Kane awakened slowly. The natural fatigue poisons released by the fading megastim were mostly gone, but enough remained to cement his eyelids and to make his tongue lie thick in his mouth. For a moment he thought he was in his shanty on the edge of the desert, fighting off the familiar hangover. There was the single open window, and the curtain hanging still and the black sky outside. Only the murmur of crickets was missing. The bed creaked as he sat up and forced his eyes open wide; peered at his watch. Twelve o'clock. He realized with a start that the door on the Chirpone cruiser had been opened sometime after he'd fallen asleep. He rubbed his jaw and wondered if the cottony taste in his mouth was really megastim reaction.

By the time he had selected some tools from the suitcase and dressed in a charcoal-colored skin suit, his legs were no longer rubbery and his head was clear. No one was in the halls as he descended the curving stone steps to Pendrake's room and wakened the alien.

"How do you feel?" he asked as Pendrake rolled a bit unsteadily to his feet.

The alien took a moment before answering in a thick voice. "I would say we have been drugged. Probably that unsavory meal we consumed in the autocaf before retiring."

Kane nodded. "By an odd coincidence the bridge door has been opened while we slept. Let's have a peek."

The streets glowed in the light of two lavender moons poised above opposite horizons. Double shadows glided on the stones before and behind Kane and Pendrake as they walked. No one else was afoot, but the windows stared like black eye sockets and Kane was glad when they'd left the streets of Ixyon to cross the field of luminescent grass bordering the space pads. They found their way to the cruiser on which they'd arrived. The telescoping ramp was extended but the entry port was closed.

They ascended the ramp and, with a tug on the door's handle, Kane verified that the port was locked. A feeling of exposure crawled along his neck in the moonlight. He ignored the feeling and studied the lock mechanism.

"Funny. Looks like a Terran model; they either copied it or bought the parts on Terra or a colony." He fished a slender, curving wire from his pocket, worked it into the hinge side of the door, twiddled it briefly and stepped back in satisfaction as the door hissed open. They stepped into the night-lit corridor and Kane palmed the door shut from inside.

They had entered the aft part of the ship, due to the vertical landing position. As they moved up the outer spiraling ramp through the cargo sections Kane saw that the holds were empty. There was a trail of dirt at his feet, probably left when the potted musal trees were carried off. A confusion of exotic smells lingered in the corridors and faded only gradually as they rose to the forward sections of the ship.

Kane had to look several times to make sure Pendrake was still with him—the alien padded along behind like a giant cat, his face a ghostly mask in the blue half-light of the security illumination. At last the narrowing spiral ended in a door. Kane opened it and looked into the well of the transverse corridor, which was used when the ship assumed its arbitrary horizontal orientation in space. Above his head was the bridge lock. It was closed; a steel ladder had been folded down to span the gap between Kane and the lock. He climbed up and removed the now bent piece of plaswire from the hinge. Then, after a moment of study, he jimmied the bridge lock.

"It makes one wonder why they bother to put locks on doors." Pendrake whispered.

"Oh, they're fine for some things," Kane murmured. He pulled himself up through the lock, Pendrake at his heels. The bridge was pitch black and Kane groped without much hope for the place where the light switch would be on an Earth ship. His finger found the switch and he grunted in surprise, flipping it on. For a moment the brilliance made them squint, and when their eyes adjusted Kane whistled; gazed slowly around the bridge.

"What is it, Elias?"

"Hasys said that the Chirpones donated an exact replica of their typical bridge to the Smithsonian museum. I'd bet my last credit that it looks nothing like this."

Pendrake studied the circular space around him. "Why do you say that?"

"Because this is a Terran bridge, my friend. I've been on them enough to know. Look at that signalman's chair—can you see a meter-tall Chirpone sitting in that? His arms wouldn't even reach the communications board. Same with the other chairs—the whole layout. I tell you it was made by and for humans." Kane paced around the bridge, his fingers touching various pieces of equipment in recognition. The five basic stations—signals, engineer, science, navigation and auxiliary control, each with its bolted swivel chair and screen—were ranged around the perimeter of the bridge at equidistant points. In the center, on a rotating dais, sat the captain's chair. The viewport above auxiliary control opened now onto the gray metal interior of the hull; when the ship assumed horizontal orientation in space, the bridge would rotate into line with the new arbitrary gravity, which was applied at right angles to the ship's long axis. At that time the viewport would match up with the clear metalplast nose cone.

Pendrake watched Kane's inspection of the bridge. "Should we not consider another possibility, Elias?"

"What's that?"

"As you say, the bridge appears to have been originally built by and for humans. However, it is entirely conceivable, is it not, that the Chirpones merely admired the design and had it installed for a hired crew of humanoids. There are many races in the galaxy with your approximate form and dimensions—I, myself, represent one of them."

"That's possible, but I doubt it. There are too many other things. I'm beginning to think, for example, that the whole ship was originally built on Earth or one of the colonies. That fact has been disguised in a hundred ways—except here on the bridge. There are enough modifications for one to think that the design is merely parallel, which makes sense. Engineering principles, after all, are not in force only on Earth. But I studied the design schematics for most of the gismos in this layout when I was in the engineering graduate program at CalTec. Oddly enough, the insignificant details, like the locks, give it away."

A visicube on the deck beside the engineer's chair caught Kane's eye; he picked it up and activated the reader. "This clinches it," he said after a moment. Pendrake looked over his shoulder at the flashing pages of the magazine. "Do you know," Kane asked, "of any other humanoid species so nearly like mine that they would be interested in photographs of nude men and women?"

"Perhaps a humanoid xenobiologist?"

"Damn it, Pendrake, this is a sex rag, not an anthropological textbook."

"I see," the alien said soberly. "It is meant for titillation rather than instruction?"

Kane smiled. "I guess that depends on the age and sophistication of the viewer."

"Curious," Pendrake mused. "I had not fully comprehended the excessive role played by the visual receptors in your sexual activities."

"Earthmen," Kane said, "or colonists. But why? How could the Chirpones trust their lives to a human crew when they won't even shake hands with us?"

"The answer may depend partly on the affiliation of the crew. If they are indeed colonists, perhaps there has been sufficient divergence from Terran behavior patterns to permit the Chirpones to trust them. Major Anders did seem fanatically devoted to them."

Kane shook his head. "Humans are humans, whether you put them on Terra or a sub-zero world at two G's."

"The truth of that depends on the answer to our earlier argument about the influence of environment on behavior," Pendrake pointed out.

"All right. So the colony environments are different. Even assuming human behavior is controlled primarily by the situation in which people find themselves, the colonies are not *that* different. The people there have human bodies; the worlds are terraformed wherever possible and artificially controlled the rest of the time. A certain proportion of colonists still lie, cheat, steal, kill and submit false income tax forms just as on Earth—before the plague. Chirpone traders were visiting Earth before all that began . . ."

"And staying inside their ships," Pendrake reminded him.

"Right. So what have the colonists got that we

haven't got? There's no way the Chirpones should be scared of us and not of them, unless . . ."

"Unless they have managed to achieve control over the colonists—or to be more precise, over the crew of this ship."

"Exactly. There's one other way it could work, too, and if that's the way it is, I've been wrong about the Chirpones," Kane said slowly. "Dead wrong."

"Unless you put your hands above your heads," a new voice said, "you're going to be just dead."

Chapter Eleven

They did as they were told and Kane turned slowly, seeing the needler first and then the head and shoulders of the man who held it. His elbows were propped on the sill of the bridge lock steadying the needler and his lower body and legs were out of sight on the ladder below. He had the tanned face of an asteroid miner; something—probably a radiation accident—had stripped away every hair from his head, including the eyebrows. His teeth, bared in an approximation of a smile, were stained red with the Inxip stick-drug, currently a favorite on Tau Ceti II. He had spoken, however, with a pure standard Terran accent.

"Okay, so we're on your bridge without permission," Kane began.

"*My* bridge?"

"A figure of speech. If you're not the watchman, why the gun? There's a law . . ."

"This isn't Terra, and I'm not the chatty type."

With a fluid motion the man levered himself onto the bridge and stood facing Kane. "You and the Cephantine are going down through the lock where my associate is going to search you. Then we will go for a trip. You will give me no trouble."

They climbed down the ladder where a short, hatchet-faced man searched Kane with professional thoroughness, giving Pendrake a more cursory once-over.

"Just a few burglar's tools, Rathis," he said when he'd finished.

"Interesting. Just what were you two after?"

"We were just looking."

Rathis looked at Pendrake. "I'm asking you."

"My companion has told you the truth."

"Just looking? That's all?"

Pendrake remained silent.

"I see. All right; Swan is going to take the lead. You will both stay at least ten steps behind him and I'll be right behind you. Move."

They descended through the spiral corridor with Swan always beyond the curvature, in case Rathis should have to fire the needler. As they circled downward, Kane considered the hodgepodge of clues. The man called Rathis was a spacer; Swan had the look of an administrator, yet Rathis seemed to be the leader. The fact that they had used names with each other was disturbing. Assuming the names were their real ones, it showed the intentions of the two men more clearly than anything else: they were not worried about being identified later. Kane nudged his mind back to the other clues.

The stained teeth spoke of colonists but the accent said Terra; teeth could be dyed and accents faked.

The men could scarcely be neither colonist nor Terran, so they had masqueraded as both; no single miscue could give them away.

They reached bottom and exited down the landing ramp. One of the two moons had dropped below the horizon and the other one had moved to zenith, trading its lavender glow–a trick of atmosphere–for a soft white. A breeze sighed through the grass around the landing field and rustled the trees beyond. Rathis pointed to an aircar which sat about ten meters from the cruiser. It had not been there earlier, and once inside the ship, Kane knew that they could not have heard its approach. He did not like the implication–that they hadn't been discovered by chance; that the two men had been sent to retrieve them.

"Get in."

"Where are you taking us?"

"You'll know that when we get there, won't you?" The man's teeth shone red in the moonlight.

"If you're thinking of abducting us onto the grounds of some embassy so I can be prosecuted for murdering that snake, Anders, the Chirpones have already cleared me." The statement had its effect, strangely enough, not with the spacer but with the man named Swan. He stiffened as if slapped and his eyes burned for a moment. He said nothing, though, and Rathis merely gestured again with the needler.

"I don't know what you're talking about. Get in."

Kane shrugged and climbed aboard the aircar. Rathis sat in back with him, while Swan piloted. The two continued to ignore Pendrake and the reason for it suddenly struck Kane. The men knew about Cephantines–knew in the first place that Pendrake was a Cephantine, knew the race's reputation for truthfulness enough to question him separately and accept his statement, knew with the confidence of experience that Pendrake would not use violence. Knowledge of Cephantines on Earth was still based mostly on rumors and sketchy journal reports; therefore, the men were probably colonists.

The aircar glided over the moonlit forest and away from the city. No one spoke and the silence lent an air of unreality to what was happening as kilometers of softly glowing treetops slipped beneath them. After almost an hour, the craft began to descend, coming to rest in a small clearing among the musal trees.

"Out," said Rathis.

"Don't want our blood in your aircar?" Kane did not move.

"You've got it wrong," Rathis said. "You were getting bored in Ixyon and you decided you'd like to explore the countryside a bit. So you and your faithful servant went into the forest and got lost, wandered in circles for days."

"And starved to death."

Rathis smiled and Kane thought of slamming the heel of his palm into the curled upper lip, against the stained teeth, driving the bridge of the nose upward into the brain. The snout of the needler prodded his ribs, as if Rathis had read his mind.

"Maybe. And maybe it'll be something quicker. Now get out."

Kane and Pendrake stepped down into the spongy mosslike covering of the forest floor and watched as the aircar lifted silently and darted away beyond the treetops. The forest wrapped them in its silence. No night bird sang, no insect murmured, no small nocturnal animals rustled through the moss. Only the short bulb-topped trunks of the musal trees surrounded them. Moonlight gilded the treetops around the clearing and frosted the peaks of the moss bed. The spicy fragrance of the fruit filled the warm breeze and cloyed in Kane's nostrils.

Pendrake gazed around the clearing. "It really is quite peaceful here."

"It's peaceful in the grave, too."

"Surely things are not that bad."

"Listen well, my cheery friend. We flew dead reckoning for nearly sixty minutes at three hundred and fifty kilometers an hour. If we started right now and walked in a perfectly straight line, we might *average* thirty-five kilometers a day through this forest. That's assuming that the terrain remains level, the trees stay this far apart, that we don't get lost, that we find water and that we can keep walking for ten days without a bite of food or more than ten hours rest a day, total. If we can find some plant life besides these musal trees, we might be all right, providing it's not also poisonous. Right now, the main thing is water. Even if we find it, we have no way to carry it with us—we'd have to leave the supply and gamble that there'd be more."

"Perhaps someone will search for us."

"Could be," Kane agreed, "but we left no tracks getting out here, and visual search won't be able to see us through the trees even if they decide to do a full 360-degree search of the forest. Maybe tomorrow, when it gets light, we'll try starting a signal fire."

Pendrake walked to the edge of the clearing and sat down with his back against a tree trunk. "You were about to say something important when that man, Rathis, surprised us on the bridge—something about having misjudged the Chirpones."

"What? Oh, that. You're thinking about that at a time like this?"

"Would you rather I thought about starving to death?"

Kane walked over and sat down beside him and looked up at the moon. "We'd come up with a theory about the Chirpones somehow controlling a human crew. I was about to say that it could work the other way, too."

"You mean that a group of humans might be controlling the Chirpones?"

"It's possible. Suppose one of the colonies decided it was tired of paying export tax on its ore and import tax on aircars from Terra. Suppose it came to resent the Earth fleets which patrol, however peaceably just outside territorial space, the presence of the imperial representatives, the status of Earth as the cultural and economic center of humanity."

"The history of your race is bloody with wars launched on flimsier premises," Pendrake agreed.

"And those wars have taken many forms, from open militarism to devious *coups*. Any colony that wished to seize control of the mother planet would have to do so by indirect means. The Earth fleet is too strong, and even if it weren't, a crucial point remains—the colonies cannot afford the physical destruction brought by a military attack on Earth. The reason is simple—four fifths of all arable land possessed by the human race is on Earth. We are the breadbasket of the colonies. There is not a single planetary ruler who doesn't know about the shielded nuclear-destruct devices planted at random strategic intervals across every section of farmland on Earth and about the red detonator button in the command silo buried somewhere two miles beneath the planet's surface. Even if their ships could selectively destroy only cities and surface command posts, the Imperator could still sack Terra with a single motion of his finger. No colony would dare the wrath of all the others with such an act, and all of them together would profit nothing from the repossession of Earth even if each wanted it for its own reasons."

"Therefore, intrigue becomes necessary for anyone who would control Earth."

"Correct. Most of the colonies are reasonably satisfied with the present arrangements—oh, there are the predictable petty bickerings between the rough and ready pioneer types and the soft Earthies who bankroll them, but a strong right arm doesn't cut off its own head. Still, there have been jealous murmurs in the last few years from some of the older and more independent colonies—Alpha Centauri IV, for example."

"Perhaps the strong right arm has begun to view itself as a head," Pendrake said.

"Perhaps. And what better way to take over Earth than to make its people kill each other off?"

"But how does this relate to the Chirpones?"

"Suppose Alpha Centauri IV wishes to bring off a *coup* against Earth. They want to do it in a way which will arouse no suspicion even if they fail. Suppose, further, that during the course of their explorations they stumble across a peaceful, gentle and somewhat backward race of traders."

"The Centauran survey ship."

Kane nodded. "They cultivate the friendship of

this race; give them the latest in space-going equipment, disguised to appear as a product of native technology. Haven't you wondered why the Chirpones, with a space fleet as modern as theirs, didn't discover Earth or one of the colonies before that expedition from Alpha Centauri IV stumbled across them?"

Pendrake nodded. "It does seem likely that a race of traders so well equipped for space travel would have discovered a lucrative market which lay a mere eight parsecs away, perhaps even before any of the colonies were founded. Of course, we are assuming that they discovered space travel well before the human race."

"How else could they have built up such an extensive trade route?" Kane asked. "But if those are really Earth or colonist ships, supplied in the way I just suggested, it would explain why humans pilot the spaceships—they do it not because the Chirpones are afraid to, but because they haven't the faintest idea how. To complete my theory let us suppose that the Centaurans offer the Chirpones space travel in return for an alliance. Suppose they implant in the Chirpones' minds the idea that Earth humans are a very violent and savage breed and that actual contact with them should be avoided. They even back it up with a cleverly orchestrated incident in which one of their men—a colonist infiltrator who, incidentally was never caught—kills a Chirpone while seeming only to touch him. They thus give the aliens a cover story which they half believe themselves and which Earthmen will accept—the notion of racial cowardice. Just like that, a backward race that once traded local goods on the surface of one mostly virginal planet is transformed into a member of the intergalactic community. More significantly, the Centaurans now have a perfect camouflage for introducing the psychopath plague. If we discover that the madness is being propagated in some way by the Chirpones—perhaps an unknown microvirus easily concealed on some popular trade commodity—the aliens are left with jam on their faces despite denials and attempts to blame the colonists. Otherwise, we wipe each other out and the Centaurans, as the nearest and strongest of Earth's colonies, step in and assume planetary control. They, of course, have either an antidote or suitable protection against whatever caused the plague."

"A fascinating theory, Elias. Then you believe that the Chirpones would be innocent dupes—carriers of the plague who were unaware of the use to which they were being put?"

"Not necessarily, but probably, yes. The unwitting accomplice angle helps to explain why a race that lives in simple buildings on a planet that is mostly forest might be involved in a scheme of planetary conquest. There are some important holes in the theory, though."

"The Krythians?"

"That's one thing. Who are they? What is their role in all this? Another problem is the trade goods. Oh sure, a lot of the Chirpone stock is artistic stuff, drugs, musal trees and exotic fabrics—all products that could be turned out here on Archepellan, but what about the Shul-Rubid tri-d device? That's a pretty sophisticated piece of equipment. The Earth engineers who've looked at it don't have a clue about how it works. It almost has to be the product of a civilization more advanced than the Chirpones appear to be."

"Could it be a new invention of one of the colonies?"

"Possibly, but it doesn't seem likely—it's too far different from existing human technology. The Shul-Rubid device is hard to explain unless the Chirpones really do have trader contacts with races beyond the present explorations of our ships."

"Perhaps the colonists, themselves, have discovered the Shul-Rubid and kept their discovery secret from Terra. Then they could have put the Chirpones in touch with the Shul-Rubid precisely to strengthen their image as intergalactic traders."

"Possibly. Possibly. There are still two big problems with this or any other theory. First, even if everything I've suggested is true—and it's really nothing more than a theory—we still don't know how it's being done. How is the entire population of Earth being driven mad in the course of a single year?"

"And the other problem?"

Kane's mouth twisted in an ironic smile. "We're sitting in the middle of a poisonous alien forest two hundred miles from the nearest town. The chances are very great that the theory will rot with our brains."

Pendrake grimaced. He looked up at the sky and Kane's eyes followed his to where the moon had been poised above the clearing. It had passed over now, leaving a patch of black on which the stars sparkled and winked. "There are worse ways and places in which to die," the alien said at last. "Ever since we landed on this planet, even with the problems we have had, I have felt peace growing in here." He tapped his chest.

Kane nodded slowly, exploring the feelings triggered by the alien's words. "So have I. It's as though getting away from Earth has cleansed me."

Pendrake turned and looked at him. "You have indeed changed, Elias. I began to sense it on the ship. If you had been as you were only days before, I believe you would have killed that man, Major Anders. And when the marine sergeant tried to coerce you and, later, the Krythians forced you to accompany them, I observed you closely and sensed a difference. I do not know if the plague has left you, but it has surely become quiescent for some reason."

Kane started to reply, then cocked his head, mouth still open, and listened. Pendrake crouched and pressed one ear against the moss, compressing it against the ground beneath. After a moment he lifted his head. "Someone is approaching, Elias."

"Someone or some*thing*," Kane whispered. "Do you remember what Esryhon said about Archepellan's forests?"

"That they contain a serpent, metaphorically speaking—a 'formidable beast,' I believe he said."

The footfalls were clearly audible now, despite the cushion of moss, and Kane could feel the ground vibrating beneath him. "I have a question," he said.

"A brief one, I trust," Pendrake said as they got to their feet.

"Your passion for nonviolence—does it extend to formidable beasts?"

A scream shattered the silence of the forest, drowning out Pendrake's reply.

Chapter Twelve

Kane ran into the forest surrounding the clearing to search for a weapon; looked back once to find Pendrake standing head down and arms crossed in the Tropos stance.

"There isn't time," Kane shouted. His hands rummaged through the moss; *damn it, where were the dead branches?* As the crashing grew louder, Kane grabbed a limb above his head and put his weight on it. The branch turned rubbery and spilled him to the ground before snapping back. He cursed and jumped up as a red glow across the clearing caught his eye. His first impression as the creature entered the clearing was of a tangle of giant tubes. Kane found himself unable to move as the animal stopped about ten meters away from him. Its round body was slung on a trio of massive legs equidistant from each other which curved upward to a height of three meters before angling down again at the joints. Kane blinked and tried to focus through the blurred corona around the body; he looked in vain for a head until one of the legs reared up and opened at the end, revealing a circle of spiked teeth and, behind them, an eye above the animal's gullet. Kane tried again to move but his feet seemed trapped in the moss. The creature saw him and ran across the clearing on two legs, while the limb with the mouth snaked forward just above the ground. Kane caught a glimpse of more eyes on the animal's body before his legs finally worked and he dodged. The striking mouth missed him by centimeters; gagged him with a gust of putrid gases. The animal recoiled and struck again, its leg-head rebounding off a tree. Kane ran through the clearing past Pendrake and hid behind a musal tree. The beast came after him, slowing as it scanned the circle of trees. For a moment there was no sound; then Kane's neck prickled as he saw the red light cast by the creature's body inching across the moss toward his feet. The leg-head slapped against the trunk just as he pushed away.

He tripped and a leg hit him between the shoulders, driving the wind out and pinning him to the moss. For a long instant he waited for the teeth to rip his back, then the pressure was gone. He rolled over, gulping air, while the creature staggered into the clearing trying to shake Pendrake off its neck. The alien's muscles knotted against the glowing skin, forcing the mouth to gape and the eye within to pulse. Chunks of moss flew upward and Pendrake grunted each time the animal pounded its leg-head against the ground. For a moment the creature stood still. Then its head dropped and the remaining two legs splayed outward. The phosphorescence flared and faded as tiny organisms beneath the skin died with their host.

Pendrake loosened his grip and rolled to the side, and Kane helped him to sit up. Shaking his head slowly, the alien looked at the cooling mound of flesh.

"If only I could have spared it."

Kane started to say something; thought better of it.

"Fortunately Esrython called the creature a beast. Otherwise I could have done nothing until I was sure it was not intelligent."

"Don't explain. I'm grateful; you saved us twice over–from being torn apart and from starving to death. There's plenty of meat here and water in the tissues for that ten-day march, if we can find a way to cut it up." Kane stopped, struck by a thought. "You will eat the meat, won't you?"

"I was forced to kill the animal; it is fitting that I renew its life in my body–that its death preserve us." Pendrake stooped and began to search through the moss. "Earlier I stepped on something hard–perhaps it is a rock which could be split and sharpened along the edge. It was around here, I believe."

Kane got down on his hands and knees to help. "A rock. I'd have traded a fortune for it a few minutes ago–wait a minute, here's something." He gripped the smooth, rounded surface and pulled, but what came up with its coat of moss was not a rock. Kane rubbed away the clinging vegetation and whistled. "It's a bone–looks like a long skinny femur."

"Perhaps this is a graveyard," Pendrake said.

"Not for the Chirpones it isn't, unless they've got some big brothers they're keeping out of sight."

"Then who?"

"It could be from a Krythian." Kane looked around the clearing, noticing again something that had nagged at his attention earlier. The pink glow of morning spilled into the clearing, making the fact even more obvious: the space in which they stood was perfectly circular. The precision was not that of nature, but rather of some intelligence. "If it's a Krythian graveyard," Kane said, "they don't bury their dead very deep. Looks more like the moss just grew over the bone."

"Here is another one, Elias." Pendrake held up a bone like the one Kane had found. Within minutes they had unearthed several more—all probably femurs. Pendrake frowned at the pile of bones. "What could have caused this?"

Kane turned one of the femurs over and over in his hands. "If I had to guess, I'd say that a party of Krythians got ambushed by Gorgo, there, and were eaten right down to their thigh bones. Notice these transverse gouges." Kane laid a bone against the animal's teeth, which were bared in a rictus. The grooves in the bone matched the spacing of the fangs. "Evidently the beast decided that the femurs were too tough."

Pendrake nodded. "A mystery remains, however."

"Correct. How did a group of professional mercenaries with blasters welded in their hands get eaten up like that? There are parts of at least six different bodies here and God knows how many more are still hidden under the moss. Unless you want to claim that they all got killed in this clearing at different times, it seems like a large gang to be taken at once, even by our late toothsome friend. . . ."

Kane stopped as Pendrake laid a finger to his lips. He heard the voices almost at once—the distant high-pitched babble of Chirpones calling back and forth. About a hundred meters from the clearing, patches of red and gold robes flickered among the tree trunks as a party of the aliens drew closer. Kane looked down at the carcass at his feet and felt relief, tainted by only the slightest of doubts.

The only way back was in an aircar from the Terran Embassy. Kane sat in the rear with Pendrake while the same marine sergeant who'd met them at the spaceport piloted the craft. The sergeant and his partner, a sunburned corporal, observed a cold silence which permitted Kane's thoughts to turn inward on his growing lassitude. Somehow, his sense of urgency was fading; the problem on Earth seemed far away and strangely unimportant. It would be nice to settle in a town like Ixyon; to live among the trees in a jade house open to perfumed breezes. He could share the evening cool in conversation with Pendrake and the traders. He could even persuade Hysrac to bring Elizabeth from Earth. . . .

He forced his mind to circle back onto his situation. Why had the Chirpones come looking for him and Pendrake without their usual contingent of bodyguards? How had they known where to look? Kane went back over the short conversation he'd had with Esryhon, the lead Chirpone in the search party. It had been shouted over a fifteen-meter distance—the closest any of the Chirpones would come to them—and had ended in less than a minute with Esryhon's promise to radio for an embassy aircar. Kane's request to ride back with the Chirpones had been rejected in high-pitched tones. He recalled the round faces peering from behind the trees at the fallen beast; what had Esryhon called it—a thrax? When Kane told the searchers that Pendrake had strangled the animal, a volley of buzzes and whistles had poured through his earplug untranslated.

The embassy car cleared the last of the forest surrounding Ixyon and settled onto the roof of the Terran Embassy, a large flat-topped pyramid of polished marble ferried piece by piece at great expense from Earth. As they climbed down and walked to the drop chute, Kane considered the most vexing question of all: if the Chirpones were really in league with the colonists, then why had they searched for him at all?

He still had no answer minutes later, when the marines ushered them onto the polished mirror tiles on which the ambassador's desk sat like a squared-off chromium iceberg. Winnifred Brace III stamped out his lunar cigar and glared at them through the green smoke as they were seated. Looking at the diplomat, Kane remembered his heavy-jowled grammar school teacher and smiled. The ambassador grunted his annoyance at what he took for Kane's arrogance.

"You've certainly caused me enough trouble."

"In what way, Mr. Ambassador?"

"Don't be cute. You shouldn't be on Archpellan in the first place. I received a sub-space message from Commissioner Clayton Tulley before your ship arrived and I need hardly quote you the charges it contained. After that you defied a duly authorized summons from the representatives of your government, burgled a Chirpone space vessel and ran off into the forest to avoid questioning. . . ."

"Hold on. We were looking inside the ship, that's true, but we took nothing and we certainly didn't run off to avoid capture." Kane explained how the two men had abducted them and dropped them three hundred and fifty kilometers into the forest without food or water. When he had finished, Brace lit another cigar and paced to a window overlooking the Chirpone capital.

"This will all be checked, you know."

"Come now, Mr. Ambassador. How else could we have gotten out so far? Is any aircar reported missing? Did the Chirpones report finding one?"

"No, but . . ."

"Just what did they report?"

"Watch your tongue, young man. I'm not under interrogation here."

Kane drew a breath. "I'm sorry. It's important that I know."

Brace turned from the window. "We're aware of your activities, Mr. Kane, and we do not approve. You are investigating the Chirpones without authorization, jeopardizing a delicate interplanetary agreement and now extending your blundering into our precarious relationship with the colonies." Brace grew thoughtful. "You *are* sure that the two men were colonists?"

"I'd stake my reputation on it. There is some kind of arrangement between the Chirpones and the colonists—an arrangement they don't want us to discover." Kane paused; decided to play the hand out a little further. "Are you aware that the Chirpone space fleet is probably piloted by colonists?"

"That's preposterous. They'd never permit such a thing. If you'd done your homework on the Chirpones, you'd know that."

"I *have* done my homework and it is true. The question is why."

"No. I simply don't believe it. You're trying to stir up trouble. I don't know what your game is, Kane, but I'm going to stop it. If you think you can embarrass your government by provoking an incident involving us, the Chirpones and the colonists, you'd better think again." Brace sat down at his desk and squinted at Kane. "That's it, isn't it? You're working for the colonists. . . ."

"Sir, it's very important that you tell me what the Chirpones said when they radioed for you to come and pick us up."

"There's nothing to that at all. When we found that you and your servant were not in the Inn of Stones, we asked the prefect–Esryhon–if he knew where you might be. He promised to conduct inquiries, and about an hour after that we got the call that he'd found you out in the forest."

"What about us being in the ship? How did you know about that?"

"That information is classified."

"What did you overhear on Esryhon's phone tap after you'd made the request to him?"

"You're on thin ice, Kane, making a charge like that."

"Just tell me this–did Esryhon get in touch with a colonist?"

Brace chewed the smoldering cigar butt a moment before giving in. "We don't know that. Our visual pickup went out for some reason. The only thing we can be sure of is that he called someone and they spoke in standard Terran."

"Rathis," Kane murmured. "How did the conversation go?"

Brace fidgeted. "Damn it, man, I can't go spilling things like that to you. . . ."

"Mr. Ambassador, we may be able to help each

other. I've told you plenty and I can tell you more, but not unless you open up."

"All right, all right. There's something queer in this, and I don't care for it one bit. Esryhon called this person—presumably an Earthman—and in a very deferential way told him that the Terran Embassy was pressuring him to produce you two."

"Had you pressured him?"

"Not at all. We merely requested. Anyway, Esryhon asked this man if he could be of any help. The man said he'd caught you two snooping around the spaceyard and that you could be found in the forest near the clearing of thrax. Esryhon thanked him profusely and the man cut the connection. I guess I must have presumed when I learned how far out you were that you'd commandeered an aircar to escape. What you say would put a different complexion on things, though I can't imagine why I should believe you."

Kane frowned. If the man Esryhon had called was Rathis, if Rathis was really a colonist and not an Earthman, and if Brace was neither inaccurate nor lying about the conversation, then it appeared that there was a secret cadre of colonists on the planet who had the Chirpones on puppet strings. Moreover, it would seem that the Chirpones had not been aware of the abduction. There were a lot of ifs and one fact that might be the key: *the video had been out on Esryhon's phone.*

"You've been prying around, Kane; what do you make of it?"

"You say this unidentified man told Esryhon to look in the clearing of thrax?"

"That's right. I've never heard of it, but they've got a native animal here—as a matter of fact, it's the only native animal I've heard of while I've been here. It's called a thrax. I saw one once—ugly brutes. The story is they're quite rare. Only ten or twelve left on the planet, each one's got its own territory, I believe. . . ."

"We are acquainted with the creature," Kane said dryly. "Pendrake killed one that attacked us."

The ambassador stared at Pendrake.

"Unfortunately, I was forced to strangle the animal," the alien murmured.

The two marines were looking at each other with raised eyebrows and Kane noticed that the flaps on their holsters were unsnapped.

"He's lying, sir. No one could kill one of those things with his bare hands."

"Don't be a fool, Sergeant. This is a Cephantine; if he says he strangled a thrax, he strangled a thrax."

Kane thought about the unsnapped holsters. He glanced around the room, noted and rejected the windows—they'd be made from plastite—and saw that there was no other door besides the one guarded by the marines. At least there was no other obvious door. Kane studied the spool case behind the ambassador's desk.

"So what do you make of it?" the ambassador said again.

Kane allowed his hands to slip onto the armrests of the chair. "A lot hinges on a man named Rathis. Do you have him in your files?"

The ambassador leaned over—too readily, Kane thought—and slipped a microspool into the viewer on his desk. "R . . . R . . . Rathis. No, there's no one called Rathis. Perhaps he used a false name—hah. . . ."

Kane leaped across the desk and tumbled the ambassador backward before the marines could draw their blasters. He pulled the sputtering diplomat to his feet with a neck lock from behind.

"Tell those men to drop the blasters. Do it now!" Kane punctuated his demand with a jolt to the ambassador's throat.

"Akk—you heard him. Drop them!"

"Good. Now tell them to leave." Kane saw Pendrake's movement out of the corner of his eye. "If *anyone* touches me, the ambassador dies." The alien hesitated and Kane hoped that the marines thought he was speaking only to them.

"Get out, get out!" Brace screamed.

The sergeant shot Kane a look of hate but the two men stepped back and the steel door slid shut in front of them.

"Lock it, Pendrake."

"Elias . . ."

"Just do it."

Pendrake walked to the door and turned the bolt. Brace peered at the alien, his eyes suddenly calculating. "You—Cephantine; get me out of this and you can go free, I swear it."

"Where's the button for your escape hatch?" Kane asked.

"I don't know what you're talking about."

"Is it under the desk? Somewhere on the spool case itself?"

"Please. It's under the desk, yes."

"You're lying. I can break your neck and still you lie. What does that button really do, fill the room with narcogen?" Kane found the carotid and pressed down hard. The ambassador squeaked before his eyes rolled up and his knees folded. Pounding began at the door as Kane eased the body to the floor.

"What have you done. . . ?"

"Just put him to sleep for a while. He'll be fine. Can you get that spool case away from the wall?"

Pendrake pressed his fingers into the narrow crack between the case and the wall and heaved. The case gave way with a ripping sound and crashed down, revealing another steel door, equipped with a double lock. Kane tried it and it wouldn't budge. Pendrake gripped the manual lock handle and leaned his weight against the door, grunting and pushing until the muscles on his neck stood out. His shoulders dropped. "It is useless. I cannot break it without the Tropos meditation."

"There's no time." Kane remembered the blasters; ran to the other door and picked them up. The banging on the outer door stopped as he returned to the hidden passage, pocketing the reader and file spool from the desk on his way. He leveled both weapons at the spot where the lock should be; the two beams converged and the metal began to glow, first red and then up through the white ranges. Heat radiated back and he squinted against the glare.

"Elias, the outer door is also beginning to glow. The marines will break through at any moment."

Kane nodded; sweat rolled down his lip to mingle salt with the acid taste in his mouth. The lock blew away into the passage; Kane stuck one of the blasters in his belt, tore off the ambassador's V-coat and wrapped it around his hands. The coat burst into flame as he pushed the blistered door ajar; he threw the burning cloth off, hardly feeling the pain, and ran into the curving stone stairwell, Pendrake behind.

The plink of water on stone mingled with their breathing as they descended. There was another door with manual locks on both sides; Kane unlocked it, pushed through and locked it again from the other side. They ran up the slight incline of a dank gloomy tunnel for a while, slipping occasionally on patches of fungus, until they came to the foot of a ladder. At the top was a trap door through which sunlight filtered in thin shafts.

Banging echoed down the tunnel; they scrambled up the ladder and Kane pushed open the trap door, squinting in the glare until he made out an abandoned stone quarry which he remembered seeing at the outskirts of Ixyon when the aircar brought them to the embassy. Chunks of the jade-like rock littered the slopes of a pit that rose on all sides around them. Kane climbed out of the shaft and motioned Pendrake to follow, closing the camouflaged trap door as soon as he was out. Together they pushed a green boulder over the door.

"That'll hold them up a bit," Kane said. "Following us becomes a sticky business now, anyway. We're out of embassy jurisdiction."

"Do you think that will stop them?"

"They'll have to get Chirpone co-operation. That'll take time; I hope it will be enough time."

"Enough time for what, Elias?" Pendrake frowned at the blaster in Kane's belt.

"Enough time for a chat with Mr. Rathis."

Chapter Thirteen

Kane stood in the hallway of the Inn of Stones, his ear pressed against the steel door to Rathis' room. Fastened above the door were punched-out metal numerals in Terran Standard and two alien languages. No noise passed through the door. Kane hesitated, reviewing the stolen embassy microfile on Rathis he'd committed to memory. Besides the address, there had been little. At first Kane had found it somewhat odd that the man should live in the same place where he and Pendrake were staying. However, Ixyon was not a large place; the Inn of Stones, which was clearly built for humans and humanoids, would be a natural choice of lodgings for Rathis. The man had never done anything of interest to the embassy—at least he'd not been caught. One entry, however, still stood out in Kane's mind: *Steven Rathis, aged 37, Captain (Retired), Royal Centauran Navy. Led expedition discovering Archepellan (Sept., '86). Quasi-citizenship granted (Nov., '86).* Two things bothered Kane.

One, thirty-seven was young for the retirement of any naval captain, line or staff. Two, Rathis had discovered Archepellan and then almost immediately renounced Centauran citizenship to live on the planet. Why?

Kane's hand settled on the butt of the blaster and he felt relief that Pendrake wasn't along. The captain would be a difficult opponent; he might require handling beyond the Cephantine's tolerance. In any case, the argument he'd used to convince Pendrake was correct—if either of them was caught, the other might still escape to carry what they'd learned to the Imperator. Kane wondered briefly how the alien was faring in his interview with Esryhon, Prefect of Police. In some ways Pendrake's part of the plan might be tougher than his, though it should not require violence. Kane shook off the feeling of foreboding. Pendrake would be all right, and he had himself to think about.

His fingers explored the door and he felt annoyance. Why, with all the trees that smothered this planet, could they not make their doors out of wood? He found the handle, twisted and was surprised when the door opened under his weight. An instinct warned him; he jerked his head back as air compressed against his throat. By reflex he snatched at the hand that held the knife and plunged forward, pulling the other man off balance and outlining him against the drawn shade. Rathis managed to get a leg between Kane's ankles and both men crashed to the carpet together. Kane kicked himself away, avoiding a second stab, and pulled the blaster from his belt.

"Hold it!"

The captain's eyes locked on the weapon and he

went very still, the knife hand still poised for a thrust.

"Just open your hand and let it drop," Kane said. Rathis did as he was told; the knife thumped on the carpet and the captain's eyes met Kane's for the first time.

"You!"

Kane studied the staring eyes; realized that the man was in near shock. "Who were you expecting?"

Rathis swallowed several times, bringing himself under control with a visible effort. Kane glanced around the darkened room. There was no vidphone. "So it wasn't you that Esryhon called this morning."

"I told you once; I'm not a chatty man."

"Even so, you and I are going to have a talk." Keeping the blaster aimed at the still kneeling man, Kane walked over to the window and drew back the curtain, letting in the late morning sun. The room was larger and better furnished than the ones he and Pendrake had rented; the chromium dresser and scoop chairs seemed incongruous against the carved jade wall. A cup half full of coffee and a plate with chicken bones had been tossed carelessly in the converter beside an autocaf unit, and the bed was rumpled.

"Have a seat." Rathis got up and settled his big frame into the chair as Kane walked over and closed the door, without taking his eyes from the man. He picked up the knife and weighed it in his hand. "I can usually size people up, Rathis. You're a tough man and I respect that. But there are some things I have to know, and you are going to tell me, because you *owe* me."

"I owe you nothing."

"You dumped me in the clearing of thrax and left

me to starve or be killed." Kane paused, taking his cue from the curiosity on the weathered face. "Don't you want to know how I got back? It's a problem, isn't it? Are you supposed to know I'm back or not? Tell me, *Captain*, who gives the orders—you colonists or the Chirpones?"

"I am not a captain and I don't know what you're talking about."

"Don't you? I presume you followed us from the inn last night. You're good; I never saw you. Perhaps then you called for Swan to join you with an aircar. After all, you had to get rid of us—we had learned your secret."

"Secret," Rathis snorted. "You talk like a child."

"Don't be a fool. I needn't be ex-navy to tell a bridge designed for human crew. You pilot the ships; I know it, you tried to kill me because I know it, but I'm still here—that's the reality you'd better accept. What I want you to tell me is why colonists are sitting at the controls of an alien space fleet."

"You keep saying colonists. . . ."

"Your standard Terran is perfect, but I've seen your file. Centauran Navy, discovery expedition . . ."

"All right."

"That was bad form, using your own name. But then, I wasn't supposed to get away from the thrax."

"There was no way." Rathis leaned forward, his voice low. "Even if you escaped the thrax, the nearest surface water was a hundred kilometers away. The whole forest is poisonous. No one knew where you were. . . ."

"No one but you, Swan and the Chirpones."

"How could the Chirpones have known?" Rathis said slowly.

"Either you or Swan told them."

"Could be." Rathis was back on balance.

"Why do you pilot Chirpone ships?"

Rathis said nothing.

"If you don't want to tell the truth, make something up—I often learn more that way."

"You're a funny man. We pilot them because the Chirpones are afraid to. It's as simple as that."

"What did they do before your little expedition stumbled across Archepellan?"

"They ran their own ships. The average lifespan of their pilots and crew was a hundred years."

"A hundred years?"

"Three hundred is normal."

Kane shook his head. If the man was lying, he was doing it well. For some reason, Major Anders' heart failure came to Kane's mind. He'd have to find a way of checking whether Anders was also part of the original expedition.

"Look, why don't you just leave them alone?" Rathis said. "You come here stirring up trouble, looking for someone to blame because the soft Earthie scum is finally choking on its own degeneracy. You've got to blame someone else, don't you? Preferably someone weak—someone different. You can't accept that the collapse of your society is inevitable."

"Inevitable?" Kane studied the captain, surprised at his vehemence.

"The last good man left Earth and went to the stars years ago. Only the weaklings—moral and physical—are left. It's no surprise they've begun to prey on each other."

"And when we finally fall apart, you'll step in and take over, is that it?"

Rathis' jaw dropped. "Is that what you think? You really don't understand us at all, do you? The destiny of the human race is not in a return to the womb; it's out there—the universe. Of course we'll send people down to man the farms if we have to, because it's that or starve. Frankly, much as I loathe you, I hope you pull through. I don't want to go back and I don't know any colonist who does. Earth is finished, whether the rabble that's left there lives or dies."

"Isn't that pretty extreme? Okay, the future of mankind is the stars, but our history is Earth. We're her children, and only a sick child hates its mother, whatever the reason."

"Don't throw that pseudopsychological rubbish at me."

Kane chose another approach. "If your destiny lies in the stars, then why have you renounced Centauran citizenship to retire on a planet already occupied by another race?"

The captain studied his hands. Kane noticed burn scars along the knuckles—more evidence of the radiation accident that left the face and head hairless. He wondered if it had been the crash-landing. "Every man has to settle somewhere," Rathis said at last.

"But you're only thirty-seven, and you were a spaceship captain."

"You know my age and my résumé, but there's a lot you don't know. You've no idea what these people are like. If you'd been taken in by them as I was, nursed back from near death . . . Well, if you knew them you'd see that they could never be the cause of what's happening on Earth. They're too kind and gentle. . . ."

"Kind and gentle, kind and gentle," snapped Kane.

"I've heard that bilge until I'm sick of it. Only the dead are beyond reproach, Rathis, and they only because they are dead."

"Spoken with true Earthie cynicism."

"Will you stow that for a minute and try to be rational? Okay, they saved your plasm, and they seem like good fellows, but have you ever put your arm around one in a bar or clapped one on the shoulder?"

"Their panic instinct . . ."

"Maybe. And maybe they just don't like you. Now why would that be? Steven Rathis loves the Chirpones so much that he gives up his roots, his ambitions and his career just to live among them. The Chirpones, on the other hand, wouldn't touch Rathis with the proverbial ten-foot pole."

"I told you. They can't help being afraid. They know our history; know how bloodthirsty and savage we are. . . ."

"You can shove that, too. Damn it, man, they've got you sniveling like the galaxy's prime quisling. Where's your self-respect? What have *you* done that they should judge *you* so harshly? That stuff about instincts is fine if you're an ivory-tower xenopologist, but there's been one thing wrong with it from the start."

"You're babbling."

"Why do the Chirpones let the Krythians up close—with blasters, yet—while they keep us behind the fence?"

"It's obvious. The Krythians are dull-witted mercenaries who do as they're told. The Chirpones control them competely, so they present no danger."

"Exactly. Can you name me one instinct in any

being you know of, human or otherwise, that depends so heavily on complex rational distinctions?"

"I'm no biologist."

"Nor am I. But it seems to me that an instinct is something which, by definition, occurs automatically—without conscious thought. Even Hysrac once told me that he could not rationally override his instinctive fear at having a human close to him. And yet Chirpones go around with packs of armed Krythians."

"Wait a minute, Kane. Instincts may be independent of rational thought, but they're not free of perception. Nothing is. If the Chirpones *perceive* the Krythians as nonthreatening, the instincts won't come into play. If they *perceive* us as a threat, regardless of logic, then their fear instincts *must* operate."

Kane shook his head. "Leaving aside the fuzzy distinction between perception and evaluation, it boils down to one question—what's the difference between us and the Krythians? Why are we threatening and they not? Is it that we have eyes instead of eyestalks, that our breath smells different, that we walk differently? Come on, Rathis. What's the critical difference?"

Rathis shrugged. "Who knows. Why does a Centauran nighteater attack a bacit but live peacefully with the wild dog?"

"How much do you know about the Krythians?"

"Not much. They come from a planet somewhere outside our ship lanes. The Chirpones hired them on as mercenaries, bodyguards. They seem very devoted to their bosses, but they stay in the background and keep their mouths shut."

"So they were already around the spaceport and

the town when you first arrived?" It was the one question toward which Kane had orchestrated the whole conversation.

"Sure."

"Where did your ship come down, Captain?"

Rathis' mouth curled. "Where do you think? Right in the middle of a forest."

"And how long was it before the Chirpones found you?"

"About three weeks. We lived off the ship's rations after analysis showed that the musal fruit was poisonous. Just as the food and water were running out, a party of them happened across us. Surprised the starch out of us—we had no idea the planet was inhabited until then."

Kane nodded to himself. Three weeks. Was it enough time to build a spaceport—a dummy spaceport? His head reeled. There were so many tangled threads. "Who built the ships they're using now?"

It was a naked question and, from the way Rathis' mouth tightened, Kane knew he would get an evasive answer. Instead, before the captain could reply, the door slammed open and six Krythians rushed into the room, blasters drawn.

Kane raised his weapon and pointed it at the captain's head, moving around so that Rathis was between him and the aliens. Half out of his chair, Rathis settled back again.

"Were you planning a surprise party?" Kane asked.

Rathis shook his head.

Esryhon stepped through the doorway, staying behind his wall of Krythians. "Please, Mr. Kane. Dwop your blaster and we'll talk."

Kane eyed the Krythians; there was uncertainty in the way they held their blasters, but all were aiming at him. His mind raced. If Esryhon was here, then what had become of Pendrake?

"Not a chance, Prefect. If your friends pull the trigger, so do I. Or don't you care what happens to Captain Rathis?"

"We care vewy much what happens to the captain. That is one weason we are here. Your Ambassador Bwace called my office not long ago. He was quite upset with you, I'm afwaid–suggested you might be planning to harm Mr. Wathis, who is one of our citizens. It appears that his concern was justified. I must ask you again to put down your weapon."

"I think we're at an impasse," Kane said. "You can't take me without risking the captain, so if you'll just back out the way you came and give us plenty of room . . ."

"You're bluffing." It was Rathis. His forehead was shiny with sweat, but he stood and took a step toward Kane. As he did, Kane noticed that Esryhon remained still; made no attempt to stop the captain.

"Odd. I know my gamblers and you didn't strike me as one. Which foot do you want me to shoot?"

Rathis hesitated.

"Mr. Kane, we cannot permit this. Suwwender and you will be tweated fairly."

"Surrender? Are you arresting me?"

"I'm afwaid we must."

"On what charge?"

"Charges, Mr. Kane, charges. You were twespassing on a Chirpone vessel, you are pwesently committing assault on a citizen of Archepellan, you slew a woyal thwax without a government permit . . ."

"What?" Kane was incredulous. "Of all the trumped up . . ."

"In addition, we have agweed to co-opewate with your government's wequest for extwadition on charges of destwuction of government pwoperty, assault on two police officers and an ambassador, theft, unlawful flight . . ."

In two strides, Kane reached Rathis; he grabbed the man's shoulder and spun him around, gripping his neck with an arm lock from behind and jamming the blaster between his shoulder blades. Reluctantly the contingent of Krythians parted for him as he marched Rathis through the door. Esryhon scurried out of the way, his voice piping.

"You cannot get away—we will not permit it."

"Don't follow or you'll lose your pet pilot." Kane pushed Rathis into the hall stairwell and almost ran Pendrake down.

"Elias!"

Kane grinned his welcome. "Can you fix that door so it won't open?"

Pendrake eyed the door, then bent the steel molding above it downward. A second later something thumped against it, but it did not budge.

"Good. Let's go."

"May we not leave the hostage? They are unable to follow."

"I've no time to argue, Pendrake."

"You will not injure him?"

"It's the kind and gentle Chirpones who are going to injure all of us if we don't move fast." Kane released his hold on Rathis' neck. "You first. Head for the spaceport and don't act stupid."

They hurried downward, the clatter of their feet on

the stone steps mingling with the banging, which grew fainter. They avoided the lobby and the veranda that enclosed the outside of the inn by using the courtyard door at the foot of the stairs. A blaster hissed against the jade wall just behind them as they ran toward one of the arches that slanted under the veranda and emptied into the street.

"Keep to the wall," Kane said. "They're taking pot-shots from the captain's window." Rathis cursed as they ran between showers of exploding rock into the protection of the arched tunnel. "Still think they're your buddies?" Kane asked.

"They've got to take some chances."

"Face it, Captain, they'll bag you in a minute if they have to. If you still think they dropped in to rescue you, then you're not as shrewd as I thought." They were running down the street now and Kane was surprised to find it empty at midday. Had the Chirpones been warned of their escape already? He filed the question; there was too much else to worry about. They reached the edge of the spaceport before they saw anyone; then a blaster beam crackled between them and all three dropped. Kane fired back and saw two Krythians take cover behind one of the raised bulwarks which served as launching pads and as docking points for incoming vessels. Kane motioned to the other two and they all scrambled behind another pad at the edge of the field.

"Where's your scout ship, Rathis?"

"What are you talking about?"

"Come on, for God's sake. They'll be coming up behind us any second. Do you want your spine spread all over this thing?" Kane scurried back as one of the Krythians who had worked his way to the side fired a shot that rained tiny bits of duraplast on their heads.

"They'd never . . ."

"Wake up, man! They're shooting at you, too. Now where is it? No space captain would retire without his own little joy-rider."

"All right, all right. It's that one over there." Rathis pointed to a gray yacht which had been converted from an obsolete Terran pocket cruiser. Another beam sliced out a chunk next to Pendrake's ear. Kane took a deep breath, relaxing his muscles and imagining that he was back at the firing range—that his targets were still only moving cardboard symbols. He rolled out and fired; saw the Krythian topple, and swung his aim to the left. The second alien was an instant too slow. Kane's shot hit its thigh and it pitched over sideways, the beam from its weapon arcing crazily. Shouts sounded behind them. Kane motioned to Rathis.

"Go. You first and get the lock open fast."

They sprinted across the port, passing between a giant tanker and a cruiser like the one on which they'd arrived. One beam from behind etched a blackened line between their feet, but the range was too extreme. Everything depended now on how long it took Rathis to get the entry lock open. When they reached the yacht, Rathis leaned against it, sides heaving.

"Damn you, open it!"

"Get slit. I'm staying right here."

Kane rammed the blaster against Rathis' skull. The man's eyes clouded and he fell against the ship. Out of the corner of his eye Kane saw Pendrake cover his face; he turned and slapped the alien's shoulder. "Hold him up." Pendrake propped the captain against his ship while Kane grabbed the man's wrist and pressed his palm against the reader. The lock cycled open. "Get him inside," Kane snapped, throwing a shot over his shoulder. Pendrake muscled Rathis up and through the lock before the steps had even extended from below. Kane ran up behind and cycled the lock shut just as a beam cut through the narrowing gap to slice his calf. The pant leg burst into flame and Kane grunted as Pendrake slapped out the fire with his hands.

"The medkit!"

"No time," Kane grated. "Got to get to the bridge." They left Rathis slumped by the lock. Kane threw an arm around Pendrake's shoulder and the alien half carried him through the narrow outer passage that spiraled up inside the hull. The bridge door was open; Kane slid into the captain's chair and his fingers hurried over the panels in front of him. "Let's hope Rathis is a proper captain and keeps her fueled," he muttered as the ship began to float upward on its antigravs. "Otherwise we'll sit up there like a balloon waiting to be punctured." The hull vibrated and the metal popped as it expanded under the heat of hand weapons. Kane flipped the rear-screen toggle and the viewer lit with a shrinking panorama of the spaceport below. Tiny figures scurried toward one of the vessels Kane identified as a light destroyer. Then the port and town dwindled to a cleared spot surrounded by forest.

"They want us pretty bad."

"Are our offenses so great?" Pendrake asked.

"You're forgetting the two Krythians," Kane murmured. "One of them is dead for sure and maybe both."

Pendrake's face paled and he rocked his head gently from side to side.

"It was us or them, my friend."

"They will surely overtake us."

"Not necessarily. We've got a good lead and should escape the gravity well far enough ahead to make a simultaneous jump and blast-off. Tricky, but possible. After that it's a hundred to one against them emerging from their own jump close enough to pick up our wake—a thousand to one if they don't have the new technetium sensors."

The rear screen now showed an expanse of wispy clouds half covering the blue-green blur of Archepellan. Kane found the neutrino scanner and punched for a readout, trying to ignore the agony in his leg. Pendrake broke out the bridge medkit and froze the wound; handed Kane a wad of gauze with which he blotted the sweat on his forehead. The scanner chattered and expelled a dot print of the volume of space below. Approximately four kilometers back and dead astern was the red blip of the pursuing destroyer. Kane calculated rapidly, then let out his breath.

"We'll make it. Their drives are twice as fast, but they can't use them until they leave the gravity well. Until then we're even up." At that moment the yacht shuddered and the planetary altimeter stopped crawling upward, began almost imperceptibly to slip back. Kane's gaze swept the telltales, froze on the flashing red indicator labeled antigravs.

"Rathis!" he shouted, leaping from the chair and stumbling against Pendrake when his leg gave out. The alien wrapped one arm around his waist and plunged into the passage leading from the bridge. Every step jolted the breath from Kane's lungs, but he craned his neck to scan the side passages. "Here," he grunted, and the alien stopped and deposited him in front of the closed drive-access hatch. Kane tried it and it wouldn't move. "He's got it dogged from inside." Pendrake nudged him aside and grabbed the wheel, threw his weight against it. With a squeal, the bolts sheared off inside and clanked to the deck. Pendrake shoved the lock open and pulled Kane into the room. Rathis stood against the bank of relays on the antigrav board, staring at the bits of twisted steel from the hatch.

"Get away from there," Kane said, hobbling toward him and cursing himself for leaving the blaster on the deck of the bridge. Rathis saw that he was unarmed and lunged toward him. Kane tried to dodge but the leg wouldn't work and he fell beneath the captain. The heavier man's weight crushed him against the deck as he tried to deflect the hands clawing for his neck. Then Rathis drifted upward, kicking.

"Please do not injure yourself," Pendrake said. "I cannot permit you to continue your aggressive actions." Rathis swung from the belt of his skin suit, chopping wildy at Pendrake's legs while the alien held him out at arm's length. Kane stumbled over to the relays and set them right again; looked for permanent damage and found none.

"Can you get him to the bridge?" he asked.

"Yes, Elias, but your leg . . ."

"I'll crawl if I have to. Don't put him down until I get there." By the time he had struggled a third of the way to the bridge, Kane's body began to float a little with each hop and his stomach felt queasy. They were nearing the lip of Archepellan's gravity well, but the damage had been done. He reached the top and launched himself across to the captain's chair in two gliding jumps, retrieving the blaster on his way. Pendrake deposited his captive on the desk and Rathis glared at Kane.

"You'll never escape them now."

"Shut up. Pendrake, tie him." When the alien hesitated he added, "Otherwise I'll probably end up blasting the fool."

Pendrake carefully trussed the captain's hands and feet with adhesive tape and settled him comfortably on the fold-down alert cot, a short bed designed for use during emergencies when the captain was unable to leave the bridge. Kane turned to the altimeter, then pressed the readout key and the auxiliary drive switch in rapid succession. As soon as the green light came on above the drive switch, he tapped in an evasive maneuver and the deck trembled as the yacht responded. He cut in the artificial gravity at two-thirds G and tore the readout slip emerging from the neutrino scanner. The red blip was much closer now—within long-missile range and closing, as the yacht's antigravs worked back up to full speed. There were four other blips, smaller than the destroyer, which were fanning out in a pursuit pattern. The on-line screens cut in automatically and Kane gazed up at them while the missiles spread astern and then seemed to veer slightly to port as the yacht's evasive maneuvers took effect.

Kane let out a pent-up breath and checked the yacht's armament. She had two small photon rigs, bow and stern, fully armed. It would be like trying to stop a charging bull with a bow and arrow. The yacht had one advantage, though: while her forward thrust was inferior to the destroyer's, her maneuverability was greater due to the lower inertial impedance factor. If he could get into position for one good shot, he might have time for the moment of deadfall before a paradoxical jump. He hunched over the controls, his gaze flicking back and forth from the screens to his hands. The destroyer was in line of sight now and closing fast on her own auxiliary drives. If he could only buy back the time Rathis had lost him. . . . He flipped the sub-space hailer to broadcast on all frequencies.

"Kane to destroyer. What are your terms?"

The receiver crackled; there was no reply. Four short static bursts told him what the scanner was already chattering. He aborted the evasive pattern and cut the auxiliaries, then sweated while four more missiles flashed across his bow.

"Secure yourself and the captain for multi-G,"Kane said as he strapped himself into the padded chair. He tilted the drives and fed them full power again, dancing to the side as the destroyer bore down on his tail. The other ship began to turn in his screens, but too slowly. Kane braked the yacht with a burst from the retros; jockeyed toward the exposed flank, arming the forward tubes as the bow of the destroyer swung toward him in an effort to cut down the angle. The instant the fire-power computer flashed green, Kane hit the launch button and felt the yacht lurch as she spat the photon torpedo. Kane stared at the screen as the bow tubes of the destroyer edged inward the last few degrees. Then a flash lit the flank of the Chirpone vessel and spun the four bow tubes out of line just as they launched their missiles. Without waiting for the outcome, Kane shut down his auxiliaries and leaned over the plotter checking the relative motion and positions of the stars on the ephemeris and laying in the paradoxical jump. Part of his mind protested as he laid in the jump. *This is madness—you must double-check—you'll emerge in an uncharted sector or in a star core.* The destroyer was limping back into position as it drifted closer to the yacht. In a second, its bow tubes could fire again, and at this range . . .

Kane swallowed and hit the master jump switch.

Chapter Fourteen

The thrust pinned Kane against his seat, forcing his lips back and squeezing his chest. He peered at the screens, which blazed with the aurora of paradoxical space. The Chirpone cruiser had, of course, vanished with the stars. That the yacht had survived the first seconds of the jump meant nothing. They might be hurtling at this moment along ten different paralines, any of which might converge in a star core. He had programed a short jump because the pilots of the Chirpone ship would probably expect a long one. Their best odds of picking up his wake lay with an intermediate jump, so the short jump seemed best. But what if the pursuers reasoned as he did? It was like the old game of paper-scissors-rock. The outcome would be known soon enough—the paradoxical aurora was already fading and the drives cut off, releasing them from the grip of acceleration.

Kane undid the straps and swiveled to face Pendrake and Rathis. The alien, who had squeezed into the engineer's chair, massaged his neck where it had been pressed against the top of the too-short headrest. Rathis was held in the emergency webbing of the cot.

"Are you going to let me out of this," he growled, waving his bound hands, "or do I stay a prisoner on my own ship?"

"What am I to do with you?" Kane asked. "If I give you the chance, you'll try to take over, and I've seen enough of sunny Archepellan."

"This is piracy."

"Grand theft. We took it from the ground, remember?"

"And abduction."

"I won't quibble."

"You see yourself as an injured victim of circumstance, Kane, but you're really a common criminal."

"That's an odd accusation coming from a man who served me up on the thrax's picnic table," Kane said, "and I'd be a victim of circumstance only if I'd let Esryhon take me. Have you figured out yet why he wanted us?"

"He gave you the charges . . ."

Kane snorted. "He tried to burn us down—all of us—when the worst charge he could trump up was simple assault. But you'll probably defend him. Perhaps he thought shooting you would be the best way to save you from kidnaping. I've got no time for this—is your brig operational?" Rathis said nothing and Kane unstrapped the blaster from his belt. "Lead on, Captain."

When Rathis was safely behind the brig's force field, Kane hobbled back to the bridge. The colors on the viewscreen were dull pink and blue-gray now—

they would know soon. Pendrake made Kane sit for an examination of the blistered flesh on his leg.

"I am no physician, Elias, but this wound could cause trouble if it is not properly attended."

Kane nodded. "It hurts like hell, but with the anesthetic I think I can make it. We'll keep it frozen and salved and worry about it if we live to see a doctor. Right now I'd like to hear how it went with Esryhon."

Pendrake pursed his lips. "I went to Esryhon's courtyard and tried to discuss the relationship of Chirpones to the colonists as you instructed. The prefect said that a few colonists had settled on Archepellan and had lived harmoniously with the native population. He showed no sign of edginess when I brought the subject around to the Chirpone fleet, and I had not yet asked him about the bridge designed for human pilots when Esryhon suddenly stood and excused himself, giving no reason. He disappeared with his Krythian escort into a room off the courtyard. Fearing some form of duplicity, I left immediately and returned to the Inn of Stones, where I met you in the stairway."

"Wait a minute, you say you left immediately?"

"That is correct."

"And yet when you came up the stairway, Esryhon had already been rattling his Krythians at me for several minutes."

Pendrake looked surprised. "Esryhon, personally, came to arrest you?"

"That's right. I'm not sure Ixyon even has any other Chirpone police official. How do you suppose he rounded up a troop of Krythians and got to Rathis' room so fast?"

"Perhaps a secret passage or some rapid form of transportation . . ."

"I don't think so. Short of a magical matter transmitter, no practical form of travel I can imagine would get him to the inn much faster than you could walk. It's only a few hundred meters."

"Perhaps the concept of a matter transmitter is not so far-fetched."

"It doesn't square very well with the apparent technological level on this planet," Kane replied, "and I doubt such an invention could be kept under wraps by the colonists."

"There are highly technological races of which Earth still knows almost nothing," Pendrake pointed out. "The Shul-Rubid, for example."

"True, but there's another problem. You said you were talking and Esryhon got up suddenly and left. Did he receive a vidphone message? Did a Krythian come in and whisper something in his ear?"

"I would have mentioned . . ." A look of comprehension spread across Pendrake's face. "Of course. How did Esryhon know when and where to come after you? Are you suggesting telepathy?"

"I don't know. It's possible that Esryhon read your mind—discovered that I was interrogating Rathis and came after me. He said Brace had called him; told him about our escapades this morning, and yet he sat for several minutes and conversed with you as if nothing had happened. Suppose he *was* reading your mind?"

Pendrake pulled at his earlobe. "I suppose it is possible. Differing forms of telepathy are not unknown in the galaxy. The Tetyon mystic castes are known to possess weak telepathy and Andinaz neuters are able to read strong masked emotions. A number of other beings and even some plants probably possess latent or vestigial telepathic capacities. Such an ability as you describe would have to be very well developed, however. Unprecedented, in fact."

"How much do we really know about them, though? If they *are* able to read minds, perhaps they are also able to drive minds insane."

Pendrake stared at him and then shook his head. "Their power would have to be too awesome, Elias. There are only a few of them on Earth. For them to create such havoc with their minds . . ."

"Okay, I'm reaching. If they were that strong and had that kind of range, it would take them about a day to do us in—not ten months. Besides, Esryhon would never have let us get away just now. He'd have turned us catatonic and we'd have come to in a dungeon—if at all. But mild telepathy is still possible. It's tough to figure Esryhon's sudden departure any other way." Kane got up and began to pace around his chair, holding onto the back for support. "Let's see. Esryhon sits and talks with you for long enough to discover the events of this morning and the fact that I am presently with Rathis—he reads it in your mind. He leaves you abruptly and comes to get me; gives me a line about Brace calling him. But no human ever shows his face during the whole episode. If Brace had really guessed that I'd visit Rathis, he'd have sent over a few bully boys, in an unofficial capacity, of course."

Pendrake nodded. "One would have expected a few marines, at least as observers, unless the Chirpones were acting entirely on their own."

"Also, Brace is plenty put out with us, but not so

mad as to give the Chirpones open season on our plasm. Much as he might enjoy that, it's too rash for a diplomat, especially given the nature of our crimes." Kane paused and looked again at the viewscreen. The colors had faded to the leaden gray of the pseudo-barrier between paradoxical and normal space. A thought struck him and he sat down. "If the Chirpones are telepaths we may be a few minutes from a lot of trouble."

"What do you mean?"

"If there were Chirpones on that destroyer and if they can read minds at a distance, they'll know I computed a short jump. They'll be able to plot the same exact jump, with time and space corrections, of course, and they'll pop out practically in our laps."

As Kane spoke, the screen flickered and went to black; the stars appeared, icy and brilliant. There was no sign of the Chirpone destroyer. He slumped and rubbed his eyes. "They could show up later."

They did not show up later. The mandatory inter-jump interval of two and one half days passed and space remained empty except for the stars. A reading of the ephemeris showed that Kane's hurried jump calculations had somehow been precise. The jump range of Rathis' yacht, the *Minstrel,* was considerably below that of the Chirpone cruiser that had carried Kane and Pendrake to Archepellan. Eleven Earth days passed before Kane readied the ship for the final jump, which would converge at a point approximately ten thousand kilometers off Terra.

By the time the ship neared its final jump point, the three occupants were near the end of their dehydrated food rations and water was running low, but the most important shortage was in the solid fuel packs of the antigravs. When Kane had checked reserves on the third day, he'd found only one half of a pack in the pod cells—an amount far below that needed for a planetfall. The retros were also low, but well enough stocked for a burn-down. The last time Kane had performed the dangerous maneuver was more than ten years ago, when he'd first trained as a navy pilot.

He sat on the bridge, the screens aglow with the final jump, and gazed at the swirling colors while he thought about Rathis. The captain had changed during the trip, from belligerence to brooding silence to lassitude so deep that Kane, fearing for his sanity, had released him from the brig three days earlier. Pendrake had been constantly at the captain's side since that time, drawing him into short conversations and urging him to eat his rations. Kane had seen the symptoms of deep depression before; it was as though removing the man from Archepellan had torn up the roots of his spirit. As the captain sat on the cot talking softly with Pendrake, Kane realized that he had not heard Rathis speak so much in days. He tuned in on the conversation.

". . . somehow I've been a fool," the captain was saying.

"Do not be too harsh with yourself," Pendrake replied. "Our existence is always a subjective matter; our lives are often shifted—our illusions of stability sometimes shattered."

"It's not like that," Rathis murmured. "I *felt* different. I loved them—I would have done anything for them, and now the feeling is gone. I can't even remember what it was like."

Kane wanted to break in, but he checked himself with an effort; Pendrake had gained Rathis' confidence over the course of days and he might shatter that bond if he tried to question the captain now. Besides, getting the yacht down required his full attention.

The jump came out as he'd calculated it and the main drives brought them in close. He followed the automatic beacon from Kennedy in New York, requested an emergency beam and began his approach vector on retros. As the ship blazed down and the blue-white surface of Earth swelled beneath them, Kane began to worry. *Why had the spaceport waited so long to activate the beam? Why had there been no verbal acknowledgment of his distress call?* The G-forces built, pushing Kane into the webfoam. Rathis grunted suggestions for balancing the ship as Kane's hand crawled over the control board with the sluggishness of high gravity. Somehow he kept the *Minstrel* centered on the descent beam—a set of bright lines on the landing grid in front of him. As long as the thin line remained centered on the thicker, they were on course. Kane glanced at the planetary altimeter—five kilometers vertical. The stern screens showed heavy cloud cover white in the afternoon sun.

The speaker in Kane's headrest crackled; emitted scraping noises, as though someone were sliding a hand over a microphone in the spaceport below. Bursts of conversation began, one speaker very loud and the other muffled in the background.

"... bastard ... know how you ..."

"... my way, or I'll ..."

"... got a ship ..."

A scream rang in Kane's ears. The ship-to-ground radio went dead and Kane stared at the landing grid where the centered lines had been. It was blank; they were going to crash.

Chapter Fifteen

With an oath, Rathis struggled out of his webbing and crawled to Kane's side.

"Get out of that chair," he growled.

Without a word, Kane unstrapped and shoved himself sideways, trying to cushion the impact of his fall with his shoulder. He slammed into the deck, clenching his teeth from the pain. Rathis muttered and swore continuously above him and the atmosphere buffeted Kane through the steel deck plates.

"Elias, can you move?"

Pendrake's voice was almost at his ear; Kane jerked his head and pushed at the deck with his uninjured leg as Pendrake helped him over to the cot and strapped him in. Kane gazed at the screen above the captain's station and weighed their chances. The ship was going down too fast, despite the steady crush of deceleration from the retros. Rathis had to keep the ship's long axis approximately parallel to their descent arc to prevent them from tumbling away from the stern heat shield and burning up. There was almost no chance of landing on or near a pad; they would probably miss the spaceport or burn-down on one of the cluster of terminals. The port swelled now in the screens, jerking as the vessel shimmied downward. The drogue and main chutes snapped open, bowing the cot beneath Kane. As the bridge heated up, sweat thinned the blood from a burst capillary in Kane's nose. He caught a last glimpse through the screens of spidery treetops at the edge of the port, then the ship crashed and the cot ripped from its frame, sending Kane downward into blackness.

He fought unconsciousness for a few seconds; sat up. Pendrake was calling his name and he could just see the alien's outline through a cloud of smoke which billowed from the con. Rathis had unstrapped and was walking away from his chair. Kane started to rise, then lurched against a bulkhead as his stomach did a flip-flop.

"We're falling over," he shouted, grabbing the edge of the cot. He and Pendrake were on the downward side of the *Minstrel* as she toppled into a stand of trees; Rathis was not so lucky. His scream filled Kane's ears as he hurtled from the far side of the bridge and thudded into one of the steel stress beams which braced the bridge cone. Pendrake clambered over the debris and hurried to the captain's side. After one look at the broken angle of Rathis' spine, Kane turned away, fighting the rush of bile in his throat. Flames crackled and the smoke began to choke them.

"Out!" Kane grabbed Pendrake's arm. "He's dead."

The Cephantine moved away from the body and they found their way to a service hatch, twisted it open and crawled into the lock. Pendrake wrestled the outside hatch open as the flames reached for their backs. They fell into a mass of scrub and struggled through, the thorns tearing their hands. Kane sank down, but Pendrake hoisted him under one arm and ran out of the trees and onto the apron of the spaceport before the ship exploded and knocked them onto their faces.

Kane rolled over and watched the flames twist upward and wondered how a man could cross parsecs of space, bring his ship down balanced on a column of fire and then die in a fifteen-foot fall. He drew a hand across his lip, smearing the blood, and turned away as the trees around the ship began to catch fire.

"Let's go."

Pendrake took Kane's arm and they walked slowly toward the terminal. In several places the burned-out shells of space liners leaned crazily or stretched on their sides, gutted leviathans. Scattered here and there among the ships that remained undamaged were abandoned service carts, some of them overturned. Cold winds whined through empty steel in what had been the nation's busiest spaceport only three weeks before. Kane studied the main control tower as they approached; the field entrance was open and the elevator lifted them to the top of the tower. Kane hesitated at the double door marked AUTHORIZED PERSONNEL ONLY. Someone inside was singing. Kane pushed through ahead of Pendrake and the man fell silent, regarding them with suspicion.

"I am the head controller," he said. "Morten had an accident, and I am the head controller." He pointed indifferently to the wrap-around observation window. A man in the torn grays of a controller lay half propped against the plastite; blood streaked downward to where his face pressed against the window.

"Accident, hell," Kane snapped. "You killed him."

The man shrugged. "He cost my promotion; he had to die."

Kane lurched forward and grabbed the man by the throat. "You damned crazy fool, you killed another man in that ship out there when you cut off the beam . . ."

Pendrake pulled him off. "He is quite mad, Elias."

The man straightened his clothes where Kane had rumpled them and frowned pettishly. "That was an accident. Happened during the fight—I'll do better with the next ship, with no one to distract me." The man paused and stared out at the bleak spaceport. "If there is another flight."

"How long since a ship has landed here?" Pendrake asked.

"Last one came three days ago. I can't understand it." The man giggled and began singing again.

Pendrake led Kane from the room. "Are you all right?"

Kane nodded. "I guess it makes sense. The controllers have a greater load of stress even under normal conditions. But what about the other spaceport personnel? Where are they?"

"Perhaps most of the people have gone to protect their homes and families, leaving a skeleton staff. . . ."

They walked in silence to the roof of one of the passenger terminals. A full fleet of hoptercabs sat in rows waiting with machine patience for fares to the city. Kane's steps dragged as they approached the nearest cab; a woman's body sprawled at the foot of it, her black hair—so much like Beth Tyson's—streaming in the gusts that swept grit and litter along the rooftop. Kane bent over and looked at her face and the bands around his chest loosened only a bit. She'd been dead for several days—strangled, by the look of it. Her clothes were torn in all the wrong places; he turned away, feeling sick. Pendrake helped him up into the cab.

"Wolcott Estate," he muttered. "Long Island."

"Certainly, sir."

They lifted and veered toward the city, and Kane saw that there were only a few other hopters. Black smoke rose from several places among the towers of Manhattan and thinned to dark smudges where the wind caught it. The hopter swept out over the island; dropped toward the lawns of the estate and the hollowed square of Beth's house. As the craft settled the last few meters, a robed and hooded figure appeared on the roof and pointed the ugly snout of a rupter at them. Kane pressed against the door of the craft but it wouldn't open.

"That will be eight credits, please."

"Oh, for God's sake . . ." He thrust his card into the slot and slid down as soon as the door opened, Pendrake waiting behind to collect the card.

"Don't come any closer!"

"Beth, it's me—Elias."

The rupter dropped only slightly and Kane moved forward more slowly. Then Pendrake stepped down from the cab behind him and Beth dropped the weapon.

"Elias—Pendrake, thank God!" She was in his arms, her hands gripping his shoulders from behind. Kane was appalled at the thinness of her body beneath the robe. He pulled back the cowl and buried his face in her hair and squeezed her until she stopped shaking; stepped back.

"This wind—let's go inside."

She brought hot tea and brandy, and they all sat together on a circular couch sunken around the fireplace in the middle of the living room. The drapes were drawn snugly and the silver chandeliers blazed despite the ample light from the fire. The brandy burned his throat and warmed his face and hands; he realized how close to shock he'd been.

"You look terrible," Beth said. "You've blood all over your face and your clothes are singed." She leaned forward. "And you've been limping; what's wrong with your leg?"

"Never mind about that," Kane said. "We're back . . ."

"And you're all right," she finished for him. "Your mind."

"I think so. At least for now. But you—you look like you haven't eaten for days."

"It's got me, Elias. I'm . . . affected. You and Pendrake must watch me every second." Her eyes fell and Kane saw that her hands were trembling. "A week ago my cleaning woman accidentally knocked over a vase. It wasn't worth twenty credits but I took after her with a butcher knife." She looked up at him. "I'm not even sorry."

"Did you . . . ?"

"She ran out of the house; got away."

Pendrake walked to the kitchen autochef and dialed a dozen scrambled eggs, some milk and fried sausage. The machine told him that there was no milk or eggs. After a short delay, it served up the meat. Pendrake turned to Beth, who was staring into the fire.

"You must try to eat."

"I'm not hungry."

"Beth, Pendrake's right."

"Damn you, I said I'm not hungry!" She turned on Kane, her face distorted. He grabbed her and pulled her close before she could react; held her until she stopped bucking against him and began to sob.

"It's all right. We'll take care of you now." Kane nodded over her shoulder at Pendrake and the alien took a plate of sausage for her, persuading her to eat while Kane wolfed down his portion. When Kane had eaten enough to blunt his hunger, he left them and went to a vidphone and punched Clayton Tulley's number, bullying his way past the subordinates and staring in disbelief when the drawn face of his old classmate filled the screen. The circles under Tulley's eyes were black and the flesh around his mouth was bloated with megastim poisons, which built up after the user had consumed a succession of doses without allowing time for recovery. The bulging lips only accentuated the gauntness of Tulley's cheeks.

"Doesn't anyone on the planet eat anymore?"

"Kane. You're back." Tulley rubbed the bridge of his nose, and for a moment Kane wondered if he'd forgotten he was on the phone. "What did you find on Archepellan?" the commissioner said at last.

"You're not thirsty for my blood?"

"Listen to me, Kane. I've lost seventy-three agents in the last week. All of the temporary holding pens have broken wide open, letting some seventeen thousand prisoners—mostly murder-one's—back on the streets. I've got corpses piling up on every corner, the city's locked up tight and the airlifts from upstate are two days late. It's the same all over the world. This blasted machine on the wall gives us all two days, plus or minus two days, before the point of no return, and you ask if I'm sore at you for slapping around a couple of agents and skipping out. That's delusions of grandeur, pal. You should have stayed away, but I'm not the reason. Got anything for me?"

"Parts of the puzzle. Maybe you've got some other parts."

"Then get in here—where are you?"

"Just a minute. How are things at the Bastion?"

"Nobody's broken us down from the outside, if that's what you mean. I've had all the blasters locked up at the exits for a week, and nobody gets one unless they're heading to the trenches, but there are still ways—one of my people just fractured another's skull for refusing to relieve him. Why?"

"I want to bring in two people with me—for protection."

"Who?"

"Pendrake and Elizabeth Tyson."

"The impresario that's chummy with the Chirpones?"

"Yes. Is something wrong?"

"We know she's the one who set up your junket, but never mind. Pretty woman, right?"

"That's right."

"I don't know, Kane. Some of my men . . ."

"Well, damn it, couldn't you put her up in your office?"

Tulley hesitated. "You seem to care about these people. Could that mean . . . ?"

"I'm clean, Clay. At least I think I am. I felt better as soon as I got off Earth."

"That proves nothing. Anyone would feel better getting out of this madhouse, whether he was cured or not. Did you know that the colonies have all quarantined us? The Arcturans blasted a liner with four hundred refugees . . ." Tulley shook his head. "All right. Bring them in. Use a hoptercab—they're still working and I can't spare a unit. Come to the A entrance and I'll meet you. And Kane, if you've got anything—anything at all—for God's sake, hurry."

"I know. Two plus *or minus* two." Kane punched the disconnect.

Clayton Tulley looked even more haggard in person than he had over the vidphone. He met them on the roof and escorted them to his office. Kane noticed the stares of some of the men as Beth passed, her hand wrapped tightly on his arm. The place stank of stale tobacco smoke—evidently a conditioner vent had broken down and no one had bothered to repair it. A pack of open ration tins littered the desk outside Tulley's office; a fistfight broke out and was smothered in the commons room as they entered the office.

Beth sat on the floor with Pendrake as Kane perched on the edge of the desk and told Tulley all that had happened since he'd left, excluding only his own theories and impressions for fear of contaminating any fresh insights Tulley might have. The commissioner stopped him only occasionally, to ask questions, and sat for a long time when he'd finished.

"How about it, Sam?" he said to the screen of the compusayer.

"Not much help, I'm afraid," the machine answered in its cultured voice. "It increases my estimate that the Chirpones are involved by only six per cent, and adds little to our suspicions that the colonists are somehow behind what is happening. Unfortunately, what we most need at this moment is not who, but how . . ."

"All right," Tulley snapped. He turned back to Kane. "I'm afraid he's right. The stuff about the human bridge design and apparent secret links between the traders and the colonists is interesting—at any other time it would be fascinating—but it doesn't turn any cogs in my head. We can't go out and arrest people with colonist visas, even if we had the manpower. I don't think it's reason enough to go after Hysrac and his group either . . ."

"They're still in New York?" Kane said in surprise.

"Come to mention it, it is odd. His ship arrived back with a new consignment a few days before you burned down. With things getting as dangerous as they are you'd think they'd avoid us, like the rest of the galaxy."

Beth got up and stared at the two men. "Leave Hysrac out of it. I've heard what you've said, Elias, and it's got to be wrong—there's got to be some innocent explanation."

"If you really believe that, you think what that explanation is and tell us. I'd like to hear it." He turned back to Tulley. "Have the Chirpones been any help? I mean, they did agree to keep their ears open on their trading runs beyond the space we've explored, right?"

Tulley nodded. "They've reported nothing of any interest. We've had them watched, though, and they're as clean as a baby's toe. Isn't there something else? Something you may have left out?"

Kane forced himself to think. His shoulder throbbed where he'd hit the deck during burn-down, and the last dose of anesthetic was beginning to wear thin on his leg. The bath he'd taken before leaving for the Bastion had made him sleepy. He labored through the familiar circles once again and came up with nothing.

"Come on," Tulley urged. "I'll bet it's locked up somewhere in that thick skull of yours. Don't be awed to silence by your betters. . . ."

Maybe it was the weariness that forced his mind to run in different channels, or maybe it was just being back on Earth again, where it had originally happened, but Tulley's remark—the juxtaposition of his two remarks, really—triggered a memory that had been meaningless and half buried: it was of the autopsy he'd seen Alfred Li perform weeks ago in the New York morgue. One scene flashed in total recall—the dead girl's head slipping out of the deaner's hand to thump on the table. Kane stared at Tulley for a minute, without seeing him. Then he smiled, his first smile in days, and it felt strange on his face.

"That's it," he said. "That's the answer."

Chapter Sixteen

Clayton Tulley stared at Kane; Pendrake got up and gripped his arm.

"What?" Tulley said. "Come on, man, for God's sake."

"I said I think I've got the answer—the most important part of it, anyway, and there may even be something we can do about it. Come on, Pendrake."

"Wait a minute. Where are you going?" Tulley stepped around his desk and barred the door. "You're not leaving until you tell me what you've figured out."

"It would take too long to explain, and when I finished, there'd still be nothing you could do."

"Don't give me that."

"I think I know what's causing the insanity, and if I'm right there's only one man who can help us in time. I'm going to see him now, and if you come along he may not co-operate—he requires special handling and he mistrusts the authorities. Now get out of my way."

"But you can't go out without protection. What if something happened to you? Everything would be lost."

"It's down the hole anyway if you hold me up any longer. You've got to trust me—you have no other choice."

"Excuse me, Commissioner," said the wall screen, "but a contingent of militia and riot police are being overcome by looters at Macy's. Agent Leahy urgently requests reinforcements. A band of former detainees from the Bronx detention camp is surrounding the Bastion and massing on Fifty-ninth mall. Also . . ."

"Hold it, Sam." Tulley stared at Kane, then moved to one side. "I'll send my two best people with you. They'll chauffeur you wherever you're going and stay in the hopter unless you need them. If you're off on a wild-goose chase, I've lost nothing. If you score . . ."

Kane nodded and started through the door.

"Elias, I'm coming with you."

Kane turned and searched Beth's face. "Yes. All right, if you're sure."

They took a catwalk over the central garden courtyard to the roof hopter area, where they were met by the two agents. One was a tall, thickly muscled man and the other was the woman who'd posed as a maid at the Alpha.

"No hard feelings?" Kane asked her as they climbed up into the hopter.

She settled into the driver's seat. "Not if you'll give me a rematch in the gym—if we get out of this. Where to?"

"You're on. Columbia University campus—Dr.

Vogelsang's house. You'd better call as soon as you've got the address and make sure he's there."

The professor was not there; his housekeeper said he'd gone to the lab two days ago and hadn't returned from the university since then. As they swept over the empty campus and dropped toward the roof of the physics building. Kane popped a megastim and fought the knot in his stomach. If the professor wasn't in his lab, or if something had happened to him, it would be almost impossible to find out the truth in time. Ironically, Vogelsang's crazy theories might make him the only man to have all the necessary equipment assembled in one place. Kane reminded himself to check the other part of it—to call Alfred Li's deaner as soon as he found Vogelsang. The hopter touched down and Kane hopped off, wincing at the jolt of pain in his leg. Pendrake gave Beth a hand down and the male agent, who had remained silent throughout the trip, started to follow.

"Uh uh," Kane said. "Tulley promised us you'd both stay put in the hopter."

The man smiled humorlessly. "And he promised me I'd go back on fingerprint-reading detail if I lost sight of you for one minute."

"Pendrake, the door." Kane grabbed the man's boot and shoved backward, while Pendrake slid the door shut and crimped the runners with two chops of his hand. The three of them ran across the roof to the drop chute. The wind had died for the moment, leaving chill air accented with dead leaves. They took the chute down and hurried through the empty halls; paused in Vogelsang's outer office to gaze at the body.

It sat, head on arms, at the receptionist's desk. Kane lifted the flabby wrist, feeling for a pulse.

"Cold," he murmured.

"Her face looks peaceful," Beth said. "Perhaps . . ."

"Heart failure," said another voice. Kane turned in surprise; he had not heard the door to the lab open.

"Dr. Vogelsang."

"Emma was with me for thirty-seven years," he continued, staring at the body of his secretary. His face was lean and the eyes bright behind their lenses. He was wearing a rumpled smock, with smudges where he'd wiped his fingers on the front. "She was a fine person. Kept things straight, kept the nuisances away. Found her like that yesterday morning."

"Professor . . ."

"Maybe it's for the best. These are terrible times." He seemed to notice the three intruders. "Terrible times."

"Yes, sir. Do you remember us?"

The professor saw Pendrake and he brightened. "The Cephantine. Of course I remember you. 'Twas only a few weeks ago. You came about my theories. Who's the young lady?"

Kane made the introduction and then explained his theory to the old man, his words tumbling over each other in haste. Vogelsang listened, tapping his fingers.

"Fascinating, young man. Don't know why I didn't think of it myself. I may have the equipment we'll need to check it out, but hadn't you better call that deaner fellow first?"

Kane turned to the office vidphone. Vogelsang seemed sharp; he'd appeared to understand, but Kane remembered how the professor's concentration had wavered during their last meeting. He found and punched in the number of the morgue, and waited while the signal droned and droned. He was on the point of punching the disconnect when someone answered, keeping the video off.

"Hallo?"

"This is Elias Kane acting for Police Commissioner Tulley. I don't know the man's name, but I must speak with Dr. Li's deaner."

"The video portion snapped on. "Mr. Kane, it's me, Karl Leicht. I'm the only one left."

Kane recognized the heavy-browed face of Li's deaner. A ribbon of blood streamed down from the matted hair to curl under the jaw, and the flesh around one eye was puffy and discolored.

"Good lord, man. What happened to you?"

"A man came. He wanted me to let him have one of the corpses—a young woman." The deaner turned and spat off screen. Kane wished Vogelsang had not moved up behind him to peer at the vidphone. "What about Dr. Li?" he asked quietly.

"Gone. All gone away. There is nothing more they can do. I stay here to protect the bodies."

"I have to ask you something about the autopsies, and I want you to think carefully before you answer, Karl."

"Mr. Kane, I am not a doctor, only a deaner—a death-house janitor, *nicht wahr?* Why ask me?"

Kane nodded grimly; the deaner's humble view of himself helped explain why the only significant observation from thousands of autopsies might not have been recognized.

"Do you remember when I observed Dr. Li at the three autopsies a few weeks ago?"

"Yah."

"You were holding up a girl's head to saw the skull, and it slipped out of your hand—banged on the table. You muttered a curse and picked it up again."

Leicht shrugged. "If you say so, Mr. Kane. There have been many autopsies. They have become all the same to me."

Kane nodded. "My question is this—why did you drop the skull?"

"I don't understand."

Kane chose his words carefully. He had to get at knowledge buried in the deaner's mind without suggesting or planting that knowledge by leading questions. "As a deaner, you handle certain tasks during an autopsy which the doctor leaves to you."

"Yah. I prepare the body, remove the brain for examination. . . ." The deaner's eyes widened. "I see. The doctor seldom touches the skull and he never lifts it, but I do." Leicht was silent for a moment, staring at a point above Kane's head. "There was something I noticed when we first started the autopsies on these mad people; I had almost decided to tell the doctor, and then I began no longer to observe it. It must have been my imagination."

"What was it?" Kane prompted when the man showed no sign of going on.

"The heads. They were too heavy."

Kane closed his eyes and let his breath out. That was it, then. The deaner had made a technician's observation which he had kept to himself, not wanting to appear presumptuous or a fool. After a few weeks, he adapted to the new weights and no longer noticed any difference. Kane wondered how many other deaners might have noticed that for a while the heads seemed a bit heavier than usual. If any of them had spoken up, none had been listened to—perhaps because the brain weight always proved normal.

"You've helped immensely, Karl. I'll try and get back to you; meanwhile, take care of yourself." Kane thumbed the disconnect and turned to Vogelsang. "Did you hear that? It's not in the brain at all—it's in the *skulls.*"

"Let's go." The professor tugged his sleeve. "Into the lab." The others followed into the cluttered room and watched as Kane helped the old man set up his equipment. "We're looking for an insulating element which could impregnate the skull and not other bones; something perhaps catalyzed by a chemical in the brain lining—the meninges," Kane said.

"A good deduction, young man. Otherwise the other bones would have been heavier too, and the autopsy weight would have given it away. Of course, there's no way to weigh the skull apart from the body unless you cut it off, which is never done. After all, the skull is merely bone—the last thing anyone would expect to cause psychopathy." Vogelsang hooked up a funnel-shaped gun with a meter in the back. "This should give us what we want."

"The element might not be any we're familiar with on Earth," Kane cautioned.

"Doesn't matter, doesn't matter. I've equipped this thing to read radiation feedbacks all up and down the spectra—used it to scan the hopter drive units when I was looking for the field that I believed disrupts mental functioning. I can see now I was on the wrong track, but at least I've got what you need, eh?" Vogelsang poked Kane in the ribs. "Not another one like it anywhere. If it's an alien element, this'll pick it up, so long as the element has any analogue properties to the Earth's periodic table." Vogelsang stopped fiddling with the scanner and stared ahead, distracted.

"What's wrong?" Kane asked.

"Problems, young fella. Unless you know what to expect in an analysis of skull bone, we won't know the anomaly if we see it."

"What if we use a negative control?"

"Ah! That's it. But who is to be the control?"

"Have you, yourself, been affected by the plague?"

"How can I be sure? I have asked myself that question many times in the past few weeks, but how could I know?"

"You'd know. Do yourself first."

Vogelsang nodded, pointed the mouth of the gun at his head and closed the contact. Kane read the analysis off the meter, writing down the atomic weights and per cent composition as each appeared on the screen. When no more numbers appeared, Vogelsang switched off the scanner and pulled down a periodic chart of the elements from its dusty roll on the wall. Working quickly, they matched all the weights to elements of the chart. None were left over.

"All right, who's next?" Vogelsang asked.

"Me," Kane said. "I've been affected at one time, but now I'm not—or at least not so that I notice." Vogelsang turned the scanner on Kane; Pendrake took over the task of recording. When he'd finished, Kane compared the two lists—his and Vogelsang's. After a moment, he found the difference.

"Here it is. Here and here. No, wait—three of them!" Kane nearly choked from excitement.

"Calm down, calm down, young man. Now what is it you've found?"

"Three new elements not on our periodic table at

all. Elements from another world." Kane's eyes flipped back and forth from Pendrake's list to the chart on the wall. "This one's 33.405, close to phosphorous or sulfur. Also, weights of 11.07 and 29.32—close, but definitely not Earth elements."

"Wait a minute, wait a minute." The old man stared at the ceiling and muttered for a minute. "That's it," he said after a moment, "It's just as you say. Elements with these weights could conceivably combine, depending on their other properties, which we can only guess at, to form a shield with high insulating properties. Why, it would be like having a coating of glass on the inside of the skull!"

"I don't understand . . ." Beth began.

"Simple, young lady. We've got elements here which may be analogues of Earth elements in which—if they are properly combined—even the outermost electrons are firmly held within the atom structure. That means the motion of free electrons—an electric current, if you like—would be greatly hampered because of strong nuclear charges. The formation process is a mystery to me. Perhaps it's as Kane says, some unusual catalytic action of the meninges. But the details don't matter. Let the pedants chew on it later."

"Yes, Professor, but what I meant was, so what if the skull is impregnated with an insulator material? No brain abnormalities were ever found."

"Of course not, of course not . . ."

Kane laid a hand on Vogelsang's arm. "It's been in the back of my mind all along. The professor planted the idea with his theory about a radiation field cutting people off from one another—although I couldn't accept the idea that the hopter engines were to blame. Trouble is, we've been looking for something added when we should be looking for something taken away. We've been approaching the problem as though something—let's say a virus or chemical poison—had been introduced into the brain, by hidden means and persons unknown, to produce insanity. What's really happened is that people have *lost* something—something that would never show up in an autopsy of a brain. They've lost their ability to feel as another person feels, to judge and to some extent *share* the impact of their actions on another. That's the only way I can describe what happened to me that night when you and I were together, Beth, and I . . ." He let the sentence hang.

"You mean we've lost the ability to empathize?" she said.

"That's a large part of it, yes; but something more is involved. People have searched for years to find out if humanity possesses any form of extrasensory perception, when now it appears that we had it all along. It was what civilized and socialized us from the beginning. What's been happening on Earth this past year is that each person has begun to pursue his own egocentric goals, without regard to other people. If someone else was in your way, you'd think nothing of killing him in the heat of the moment. Before, we cared about other people—whether we knew it or not—because we shared a mass experience. The madness started when we lost this ability—were literally insulated from each other." While Kane was talking, Vogelsang completed a reading on Beth and Pendrake and whistled.

"This young lady's got it too—much more of it, by a factor of at least twenty. You, Cephantine, you've got a totally different group of elements, along with some shared ones, but none of the three that showed up in Kane and the young woman."

"That makes sense," Kane said. "Pendrake has never been affected."

Beth shook her head. "You're telling me that caring about each other has come from . . . from some electric current passing between all of our brains?"

"It looks that way," Kane said. "And why not? We've known for years that people put out electrical auras, but no one's ever been able to assign a purpose to those auras. It seems mystical only because the notion is brand new. Of course, this *is* still a lot of guesswork."

"Nevertheless," Pendrake said, "we have something to go on, regardless of the ultimate explanation. We have found a difference that should not be there."

Beth raised her hands to the sides of her head and frowned. "But wouldn't I notice it if my head got heavier?"

Kane smiled. "Not if it happened gradually."

"All right. Suppose you're correct. There are still a million questions. How was it done, why and by whom?"

"I've got some ideas about that, too," Kane said. "But first we have to deal with the toughest question of all—can we do anything about it?"

Chapter Seventeen

Silence stretched in the lab. Vogelsang paced up and down, his smock flapping, and Kane stared out the east wall of the lab, which was polarized for viewing. The campus was empty; empty in October when it should have held thousands of students with problems like preparing for midterms, planning a conquest or wringing a bigger credit balance from home. Instead, bits of trash blew across the unmowed quadrangles under a gray sky. One of the nearby buildings was a gutted shell—the chemistry building, Kane guessed, by the look of the debris.

"It would help if we had some idea how it was done," muttered Vogelsang.

"By some form of radiation plating, I'd guess," Kane said. "It sounds far out, but a group at Universal was playing with something like that a few years ago. Remember, we're dealing with an alien technology here. The effects seem very much like those of electroplating, except that the air is substituted for a fluid medium and nonmetallic elements for metals. It sounds impossible, but *something* caused that layer of insulation, and none of us has had our skulls opened."

The professor stopped pacing and leaned against the table. "If you could only have been my student," he said softly. "It's crazy and it's right. I should have been the one to think of it." His voice sounded very old.

Kane tried to think of something to say—something to keep Vogelsang from growing despondent at a time when his full powers were so urgently needed—but no words would come except those that might patronize.

"No matter. No matter. That gives us our answer."

"It does?" Beth said.

Kane looked at Vogelsang. "Bombardment to cause nuclear disintegration."

"Correct," the professor said. "But which kind? Alpha particles? High-speed protons? Deuterons? Neutrons? Besides, it could be dangerous. What if the energy becomes too great or we knock apart the wrong atoms? Why, it could turn your skull to mush."

"We've got the atomic weights for a start; we'll have to estimate the other properties on an analogue basis and tailor the bombarding field accordingly."

"But the danger . . ."

"If we don't try, we're finished," Beth said quietly.

Vogelsang nodded.

The two men worked quickly, building the small field gun while Pendrake and Beth watched. They had almost finished—Vogelsang was carefully inserting the nuclear core—when something clattered in the office outside the lab. Kane's eyes met Pendrake's and the alien nodded; moved over to the door. He gripped and held the door knob while the rest of them waited, keeping still. There were sounds of a search in the office; after a silence, Pendrake stiffened and Kane saw his knuckles whiten on the door handle.

"We know you're in there. Give yourselves up and you won't be harmed."

"Professor," Kane whispered. "Can you finish this?"

Vogelsang nodded.

"Good. As soon as you're done, you and Beth take a hoptercab to the ImpSec bastion. Say you have vital information for the commissioner. Try not to show the gun unless you have to; just get to Tulley's office somehow. Say you have information about me and what I discovered that he'll find valuable. Say anything that works."

"But what about testing . . . ?"

"Please don't ask questions. There isn't time. Just get it finished and come as soon as you can." Kane turned to Beth. "Will you see that he gets there?"

"We'll manage it between the two of us. We'll get in however we have to."

"Good. Now, is there someplace where the two of you can hide?"

"Open up or we'll blast our way in."

Vogelsang looked around. "The closet?"

"It'll have to do. Get going."

When they were out of sight, Kane nodded at Pendrake, who released the door, allowing two men to stumble into the room. Behind them was the big agent they'd left in the hopter, and in his hand was a blaster set to wide beam.

"That was a cute trick your orange-headed pal pulled with the door, Kane. Maybe you've got some others, like stopping a bolt from this with your hands." He gestured with the blaster.

"You're being a fool."

The man's smile slipped. "Where's Ms. Tyson?"

"I sent her out to look for the professor. We're waiting here in case he shows up at the lab."

"That crazy bird? He's probably out hexing hopters with his secret ray gun. Get moving."

One of the other agents asked, "Hey, Rooker, shouldn't we look for the woman?"

"Nope. Tulley said nothing about her. He wants these two, and fast. You gonna move or do I heat up your feet?"

Another hopter had landed beside the first one, which now sported a gaping hole where the door should have been. The woman had switched to the new hopter and was waiting at the controls; as soon as they'd boarded, the man called Rooker patched the vidphone through to Tulley.

"We got 'em, Chief. They were in Vogelsang's lab."

"Now I know he's crazy. Bring them in."

Kane leaned across in front of the pickup. "Clay, will you listen for one minute . . . ?"

"Shut up." Rooker shoved him back.

"Hold on. Make it fast, Kane."

"You've got to let me stay."

"No chance. I don't like games—you interfered with one of my people. I've got no idea what you're up to, and you know something you won't tell."

"Damn it, Tulley, I know how to stop the plague—how to reverse it!"

"I'm impressed. Get in here and whisper it to Uncle Clay before you do another thing."

"You insist on bringing me in?"

"Absolutely."

"All right. I want you to do something right away. I want you to call a meeting."

"Fine. It's a nice day for meetings. Let's see, who shall I invite?"

"For God's sake, Clay, I'm serious." Kane tried to think of a lever that might move the man. "Do exactly as I say and you'll be a good bit more than eastern sector commissioner within the week. If you foul up a single particular, it's all over—for all of us."

Tulley paused, assessing. "All right, but you're coming straight here. Nothing you say can change that. And if this is some ploy, you won't even live as long as the rest of us. Now what is it you want me to do?"

When they landed on the Bastion roof, Kane could see the wall of rioters pressing in on all sides. Occasionally a blaster flared, and the wind carried snatches of screams up to the rooftop. Smoke billowed a block away, and crimson fire-fighting robots wailed and dipped over the flames. The agents ushered them into the quiet of the Bastion, led them to Tulley's office, taking up positions by the door when the commissioner did not dismiss them.

"Do you really want them to hear all of this?" Kane asked.

Tulley frowned and motioned them out; Rooker and one of the others remained just outside the door.

"Now tell me everything."

"Did you call the meeting?"

"Yes. It took some doing, but when I told them I had the solution, the Imperator himself agreed to come." Kane did not miss Tulley's use of "I." "He's on the shuttle from Washington right now," the commissioner continued, "along with his top aides. The other commissioners and deputies are en route, too. The meeting is scheduled in one hour in the main conference hall. So help me, Elias . . ."

"How about Hysrac?"

"Yes, yes. He's already waiting in a side room with those stick-figure bodyguards of his, and the colonial ambassadors are all on their way, just as you asked. I've put my skin on the line for you, because I know how clever you were once, and because it won't speed my fate if you're conning me–only yours. Now give it to me from the top."

The vidphone flashed red. Tulley growled and snapped on the privacy earphones. "Damn it, I said no calls . . . Yes . . . yes, I see. All right, I'll come right over." He flipped off the earphones and stood. "I'll be right back. You will wait for me, won't you?" Tulley looked pointedly at the men outside the door.

"May I ask where you're going?"

"No."

"Clay, nothing's more important or more pressing than what I have to tell you."

Tulley paused with his hand on the door. "Nothing–except perhaps for another explanation of the psychopath plague from a more reliable source."

"A more reliable . . . Clay, wait!"

But the commissioner was gone. When Kane hurried after him he found his way barred by Rooker; reluctantly, he returned to his seat by the desk.

"Commissioner Tulley seems unconvinced that you have the answer," Pendrake said. "There seems to be a higher bidder."

Kane nodded. "Yes, but who? Is it possible that one of his own experts has independently come up with the same answer?"

"For the sake of your people, I hope so. Time is short."

Even as Pendrake spoke, the compusayer clattered to life. "Commissioner Tulley, excuse me, but you directed that I break in with updates on the Russian insurrections. Commissioner?"

"He's out."

The blue visual monitor snapped on and the compusayer identified the voiceprint. "Thank you, Mr. Kane. I shall put myself on body ident monitoring so that I will be activated when the commissioner returns. You need have no fear for your privacy." The blue eye scanned first Kane then Pendrake and snapped off again.

"A fascinating machine."

"Within a week, it may be the last intelligence left on the planet."

"Elias, I have been thinking; trying to decide who is behind the destructive process you have discovered. The most likely source of the plague appears to be the colonists, and yet I find that conclusion difficult to accept. I talked briefly with Captain Rathis just before he died."

"I know. What were your impressions?"

"That he, at least, was not part of any conspiracy against Earth. His worst mistake appeared to be a fanatical devotion to his adopted planet."

"If only we could have questioned him further," Kane said.

"Then you, too, are still uncertain about the conspirators' identities?"

Kane massaged his temples. The megastim he'd taken on the way to the lab was still working, but the metallic taste in his mouth told the price he would pay later. His leg throbbed just below the level of pain and his eyeballs felt too dry, as if the wind had been blowing on them. "Pendrake, it's all in here," he said, tapping his forehead. "Everything I need to piece it all together. If only I had time to think."

"Do you believe it is the Chirpones?"

"I've suspected them all along; there's plenty that's not right about them; plenty that doesn't meet the eye. But there's also still that one glaring inconsistency."

"Motive."

"Exactly. There's just not a single reason I can think of why they'd want to do us in."

"Perhaps it is a pre-emptive strike. They possess a nearly virginal planet; knowing the acquisitive history and nature of your race, they may wish to ruin Earth before Earth has a chance to destroy their culture."

"That would be reasonable except for one thing—the colonists. The colonists are much closer to Archepellan. Moreover, they are precisely that group of humans which is, by definition, most likely to take over Archepellan. And yet, the Chirpones live quite amicably with them."

"Still, the colonies depend heavily on Earth for their basic food staples. To strike at Earth would be to deliver a crippling blow to the colonies as well . . ."

"Practically ensuring that the colonies would annex Archepellan," Kane pointed out.

"I do not understand."

"It would be a natural choice—it's clearly a fertile

planet. I'm no botanical expert, but those trees don't look too different from basic Earth plants. I'm betting the planet could be cleared in nothing flat and planted over with wheat, soy beans—what have you. And another thing. I'm not at all sure the colonies are going to be dependent on us for food in the future. They may have discovered several planets suitable for farming already, and are hiding their finds so that Earth doesn't try to extend its monopoly."

"Why do you say that "

"Two reasons. The first is common sense. We know their number one priority has been a search for arable planets; sooner or later they're likely to find them. Secondly, the quarantine."

Pendrake frowned and then nodded slowly. "Of course. Not only have no colonists landed, despite the fact that your planet is hardly in a position to resist, they have also refused all Earth ships any access to their worlds. How, then, are they getting food?"

"From somewhere else. So you see, it just doesn't pay the Chirpones to attack us."

"If what you suggest is true about the colonists finding new food, their motive for attacking Earth would also appear to diminish," Pendrake pointed out.

"True, and yet the evidence remains. The colonists and the Chirpones are playing footsie, and Esryhon did his best to finish us for reasons I ought to know but don't. He was afraid that I found out something damaging during my stay on Archepellan—something so threatening that he stepped way out of Chirpone character to try to stop us from getting back here. That something must be floating around in little pieces inside my brain right now, if only I could figure it out. But first we've got to get the plague reversed." Kane glanced up at Tulley's wall clock. "Vogelsang should be finished by now; perhaps even on his way over here."

"What if the device does not work?" Pendrake asked.

"Then we'll have to modify it until it does, and hope we solve the problem in time." Kane fiddled with some papers on the commissioner's desk. "What the devil is keeping Tulley? I don't like the smell of this . . ."

Just then, the commissioner appeared outside the door and nodded to Rooker, who opened it for him. He walked in and settled himself at his desk.

"Well, Kane, it appears that I have no need of your theories. I know what is causing the psychopath plague."

"What is it and who told you?"

The commissioner held up his hand. "I'm not answerable to you. In fact . . ."

Rooker rapped on the plastite and Tulley waved him in. Behind him, escorted by a pair of agents, were Vogelsang and Beth Tyson. Kane's eyes met hers; tried to read their message. Neither of them was carrying anything at all, let alone something that could be the nuclear disintegrator.

"These two landed on the roof," Rooker said. "Claimed they had special information for your ears only."

"Fine, fine." Tulley gestured expansively. "This rounds things out very nicely. Take all of these people down to sub-level four and lock them up. Use the old cells—we wouldn't want a power failure setting them free."

"Clay, for God's sake, you can't . . ."

"Shut your mouth and get moving." Rooker grinned and jabbed Kane's back with his blaster.

Vogelsang drew himself up stiffly. "Young man, I demand to know the charge."

"Certainly," Tulley said. "The charge is high treason."

"That's rubbish and you know it," Kane said.

"Do I?" Tulley answered. "I admit, it was a good ploy, persuading me to call together all the big hats. What was it going to be? A leathol capsule in the ventilation system, or a fingerbomb planted during one of your visits? We're having the council chambers searched; we'll have our meeting all right, and I'll expose your whole scheme."

"You're crazy. Where's my motive?"

"You just returned from Archepellan, where you kept a rendezvous with the leader of a colonist plot against Earth and the Imperator—a man named Rathis, who was using the Chirpones as cover."

"If you believe that . . ."

"Rathis was killed in your crash-landing, but you were prepared to finish the job you started when you first introduced the microvirus from Alpha Centauri IV eleven months ago. You'll be interested to know that a cargo of antidote is now en route."

"A *virus!* And why, in God's name, would I involve myself in a scenario like that?"

"Money, of course. Always was your weakness. I wondered how you could show up here decked out in such finery and having just gambled away four hundred thousand credits."

Kane stared at the commissioner; felt the agent's grip on his arm. "Clay, it's me, the same guy that saved your life ten years ago."

Tulley shrugged. "People change, Elias. No one's sorrier than I am. Take them away."

Kane hardly noticed as they were prodded and pushed to the drop shaft and then led through a maze of dim subterranean corridors that smelled of dampness and mold. They were herded into a tiny cell and the iron door clanged shut behind them.

"This is outrageous," Vogelsang said. "Do you expect the three of us and a lady to remain in this . . . this medieval place? Why, there are no beds. And are we all to share that?" Kane's eyes followed the shaking finger that pointed to the sink and bare toilet which sat in a corner, but his thoughts were far away. *He knew. He knew everything there was to know—every piece had fallen into place. But was it too late?*

"Shut up, old man," Rooker was saying. "If I were the commissioner, I'd have burned you all down on the spot." He twisted the key in the old-style lock and motioned for the escort to follow him. When the footsteps died away, Vogelsang turned on Kane.

"These trumped-up charges—what did you do to the man that he wants to destroy you?"

"Then you don't believe him?"

The professor snorted. "It was my lab we worked in, remember? My old brain takes occasional excursions, but so far it's always returned. Now we're finished. We can never get the disintegrator into operation. The planet is doomed."

"The disintegrator. Where is it?"

"Right here," Beth said. She lifted the hem of her

ankle-length skirt and unstrapped the nuclear gun from her leg. "I was sure they were going to search me, but everything happened so fast . . ."

Kane accepted the gun; hugged her. "There may be hope yet."

"I don't see how," Vogelsang muttered. "These walls are solid plascrete, we're so far underground no one could even hear us scream and as for those bars . . ."

Kane pressed his face against the cold iron and peered down the corridor to the room with the lead-shielded walls and the massive overhead ruptors. A spy lens in an upper corner would relay their deaths to those who could watch a human being destroyed cell by cell. Kane knew without any doubt that the order would come from Tulley's office at any moment.

"Pendrake, is something wrong?" Beth asked.

Kane turned and glanced at the Cephantine, who was standing in a corner, eyes glassy and arms folded. "Don't disturb him," he said. "We haven't much time. Professor, is the gun ready to use? Professor . . ."

"Eh? Mustn't wake Emma." The old man's eyes were far away and his shoulders had caved inward. He leaned against the plascrete and slid down to his haunches. "She's worked so hard; deserves a rest, poor soul." He trailed off into mumbling and Kane shook his head.

"The gun's finished," Beth said, "but it hasn't been tested. I think we should use it on me, right now."

"That's out of the question," Kane said.

"Why?"

"Too dangerous. We had only guesswork to go on . . ."

"Stop that, Elias. I know it's dangerous. The room at the end of the hall is fatal—yes, I noticed it too. I don't see that using the gun makes much difference."

"We're not going to die in that room. We're getting out of here."

She smiled sadly. "I don't need protecting. In spite of everything, it's been good. I'd like to go out with my brain the way it was. I want to know how I *feel* about you; you can't take that chance away from me."

With Pendrake locked in the Tropos trance and Vogelsang talking quietly to himself on the filthy floor, Kane aimed the gun at her head and closed the contact.

She winced. "No, don't stop. Feels funny. My nose itches." Then she cried out and fell to her knees. Kane shut off the gun and knelt beside her. "Oh, Elias, it's gone." She gripped his hands tightly. A door slammed somewhere far down the corridor. The Imperator and the others must have arrived already; the cameras in the execution chamber would relay their punishment to the council room. *This is how we deal with treason, Imperator.* Kane could not yet hear the footsteps, but he knew they were coming. Pendrake stirred and walked to the door.

"See what you can do for the professor," Kane said; Beth nodded and hurried to the old man's side. Kane picked up the gun and joined Pendrake at the door. The alien gripped two adjacent bars, and his elbows extended outward. His back strained and the muscles swelled, drawing the fabric of his tunic tight. At first the bars did not move, but then they began to inch apart. The metal groaned and popped as it gave way, almost drowning out the approaching steps.

"What the devil!"

Kane turned and saw the professor staring at Pendrake, his eyes sharp once more. Beth also gaped at the alien as she helped Vogelsang to his feet.

"We'll run into the room at the end," Kane said. Beth nodded; the professor brushed her hand off his arm and walked to the door. With a last creak, the gap widened out to the next set of bars. Kane tapped Pendrake on the shoulder.

"It'll have to do. You first—if you fit, so will the rest of us. Quickly."

Pendrake pushed into the opening. For a moment, as the footsteps approached the last bend in the corridor, it seemed that the alien was caught. Then he squeezed through and the others followed, slipping into the execution chamber and ranging themselves on either side of the entrance, out of sight from the corridor. The steps halted in front of the cell and someone swore. "It can't be!"

"Silence, you idiot." It was Rooker's voice. "You three, get back up the shaft and fan out to the ground-level exits. Sound the alarm. Payte, stay with me."

Kane listened as some of the men moved off. There was nowhere for Rooker to search but the execution chamber; boot leather creaked a few meters away. Kane's hand tightened around the grip of the disintegrator. It would have to be played just right.

"Don't shoot, Rooker, I'm coming out." Kane gave them just enough time to react before he stepped into the doorway, holding the gun loosely. Rooker stiffened and aimed his blaster.

"Drop it," the agent said.

"Sorry. Even if you shoot me, this'll eat you up where you stand, and half the corridor besides. Anyway, there are three more of us and we're all armed."

The two men stared at the device in Kane's hand. "You're bluffing."

"Maybe. Why not be a hero? Of course, then you'd never know if you were right."

The blaster of Rooker's partner wavered.

"Three seconds," Kane murmured.

The weapons clattered to the floor. "You'll never get out anyway, Kane. The exits are sealed."

"Who said anything about leaving? Pendrake."

The Cephantine and the other two stepped out of hiding.

"Don't you think you should fix those bars?"

"Yes, Elias."

"*After* you've relieved Mr. Rooker of his key and escorted him and his friend inside. Get their comwebs, too, while you're at it."

While Pendrake bent the bars back, Kane pocketed the small two-way communicators and collected the weapons; gave one to Beth and kept the other and a small stunner that had been hidden in Rooker's boot for himself. He turned to the cell; the two men were staring at Pendrake.

"The council room, Rooker; where is it?"

The man frowned at the blaster. "Across the courtyard from the commissioner's office, same level, but you'll never get in."

"And the room where the Chirpones and Krythians were waiting?"

"There's a bunch of small committee rooms in the

corridor outside. I don't know which one—wait, Kane, before you go. About that funny weapon of yours?"

"This little thing?" Kane pointed the gun at Rooker's head and closed the contact.

"Damn you, it wasn't . . ." Rooker rubbed at his nose and shook his head as if to clear it. Then tears began to roll down his cheeks.

"Rooker!" said the other man in amazement.

"Leave me alone," the agent said softly.

Kane led the others down the corridor and signaled a halt when they reached the drop shaft.

"What next?" Vogelsang asked. Kane outlined his plan. The professor shook his head in wonder.

"You're sure about this?" Pendrake asked.

Kane shrugged. "All life is a gamble." He turned to Beth. "Are you set for your part?"

"Sure. I hide out in the courtyard garden and listen to you on the comweb; stay ready for your signal. But I wish you could explain."

"There's no time. Dr. Vogelsang, you stay with me. Let's go."

They rode the drop shaft to the top levels and surprised two agents who were passing in the corridor when they stepped out. Fortunately, Tully had revoked weapons from the staff days ago. The group split up according to plan; Kane kept one of the agents as a hostage and hurried through the hallways to the council chamber, with Vogelsang trailing behind. No one tried to stop them, though some followed at a distance. Two marines with ruptors were braced at attention outside the gleaming doors of the chamber. Their stiff dignity cost them seconds; Kane toppled both with a blanket spray from Rooker's stunner. He pushed the hostage ahead of him into the council chamber.

His entrance into the square, polished room seemed to catch everyone but Cayton Tulley and Hysrac by surprise. The commissioner turned to stare at him, but the Chirpone trader did not even look his way. The other commissioners and their aides gazed at him from their tables along the chrome-plated walls and even the Imperator, attended by his black-suited praetorian guard and a retinue of courtiers, uttered an unimperial oath of surprise. The circle of Krythians that separated Hysrac from the others in the chamber drew their blasters.

The commissioner said, "Give yourself up now, Kane, and there may be mercy for you."

"If you're through," Kane countered, "I'd like to speak. When I'm finished, I'll have no need of mercy."

"Guards, take that man by whatever means necessary."

Kane pulled the frightened hostage closer.

"Belay that," boomed the Imperator in a voice befitting an ex-admiral of the fleet.

"Imperator, I was only thinking of your safety."

"My praetorians will see to that," the old man said dryly. "Is this the man about whom you have been exhorting us?"

"Yes, Imperator," Tulley said.

"Come closer. You, old man, stay where you are."

Kane threw down his blaster and walked forward to stand in the center of the room. The Imperator glared from beneath the famed white-tufted eyebrows. The brown face had not paled in the days since his fleet had consolidated the warring factions of Earth into one strong government. At his signal, two praetorians nearly the size of Pendrake detached themselves from the guard and walked over to stand on either side of Kane. One inspected the nuclear disintegrator with a scanning device and then handed it back to Kane with a bored look.

The Imperator cleared his throat. "You have been accused of a heinous crime—a plot against ourselves and all of the empire. A plot that even now has brought an insane mob to crush against the walls of this Bastion. No one in history has ever faced a charge of such magnitude. What have you to say for yourself before I abandon you to the sport of the commissioner?"

"That I am innocent."

"Naturally. And what else?"

"I have come to collect the million credit purse you offered to the one who could discover the cause of the psychopath plague."

The Imperator snorted. "You're a cheeky one. Commissioner Tulley has already offered us the solution."

"Has he also offered you an immediate cure?"

"A suitable antiviral serum is on its way."

"From Archepellan?"

"That is correct."

"Imperator, there is no microvirus, the Chirpones are scarcely capable of producing an antiviral serum in any case, and even if they could, it would never reach Earth in time, let alone act with sufficient speed." Kane's eyes moved to the doors of the chamber and back. *What was keeping Pendrake?*

"Those shortcomings have not escaped my attention," the Imperator said. "You offer us an alternative?"

"Imperator, I have known this man for some time," Tulley broke in. "As you have already seen, he is loyal only to money. He is guilty of everything I have charged . . ."

"Commissioner, I addressed myself to Mr. Kane," the Imperator said, not unkindly. Tulley bowed sullenly.

Kane turned on his old friend. "You say you have known me for some time. Then perhaps you can tell your colleagues and the Imperator about the time I saved your life."

"That is of no relevance here."

"It is of every relevance. The worst I ever saved you from was flunking an exam."

Tulley did not look at him but seemed to stare off at a point somewhere above everyone's head. "I assumed you were speaking figuratively, of course."

"It was in Dr. Glover's class. You do remember your major professor, don't you?"

"There . . . there was never any Dr. Glover."

"Ah, but there was. Shall we have your compusayer fax the records?"

"He's lying, Imperator—deliberately trying to confuse you."

"I am not the one who is confused, here, Commissioner Tulley . . ."

The door to the chamber banged open and every eye swung around, and Kane felt weak with relief as Pendrake walked in. On one arm he supported the tottering figure of Clayton Tulley.

Chapter Eighteen

"What the devil is going on here?" said the Imperator after a moment of stunned silence.

"Imperator, it is obvious that Kane has brought in an imposter to support his wild claim—someone pretending to be me . . ."

"Nothing is obvious here."

"Imperator, I can explain everything," Kane said.

"I insist . . ."

"*You* insist?" The Imperator glared the first Tulley to silence, then nodded at Kane. At Kane's signal, Pendrake helped the second Tulley down the steps and the three of them stood together. Both of the commissioner's eyes were black and a huge lump swelled his forehead on one side. He put a hand on Kane's shoulder and groaned.

"Where did you find him?" Kane whispered.

"Trussed up in one of the committee rooms, just as you suggested," Pendrake said. "In his run-down condition it took me nearly a minute to revive him."

Kane turned to Tulley. "The Krythians?"

"That's right. The Chirpones lured me out of the office; told me they had information on the plague and proof that you were a traitor—that I must see them before I listened to you. How in hell they even knew you were here I don't know. Anyway, when I got there, one of those skinny brutes they keep as pets punched me out with something heavy. Next thing I knew, your valet here was cuffing my face. What's it all about, Elias? And who the hell is that ringer?"

"Mr. Kane, we await your clarification."

Kane patted his friend on the shoulder and turned to face the Imperator. "I told you I had solved the psychopath plague and I have. These two Commissioner Tulleys—beside me the real one and over there the imposter—are part of the proof. Since the truth about who is real and who is fake will emerge as a matter of course, I will begin with the part you most need to know. The psychopath plague is the work of the Chirpones."

"Impewator, as wepwesentative of a foweign and soveweign power, I pwotest this flagwant pwovocation." Heads turned at the first words spoken by the Chirpone; Kane saw that the Krythians had not holstered their blasters since he had come in, and that their weapons were loosely pointed at him. To one side, the first Clayton Tulley stood very still. The Imperator fixed Hysrac with a calculating look.

"On the one hand," he said, "I appreciate your desire to protect your reputation, but you must also understand our position. Humanity has suffered great and perhaps irreversible damage from the plague. At this late hour we must explore all possible explanations and all possible solutions. I assure you, if Mr.

Kane's accusations are false, he will suffer the full extent of my anger; however, I must first hear and evaluate his statement, no matter how wild it may seem. Mr. Kane, you say the Chirpones are responsible. How?"

"As Dr. Vogelsang and I discovered earlier today, the madness is caused by irradiation with alien elements which form an insulating layer inside the skull."

"That is absurd," Hysrac said.

The Imperator remained polite. "I must judge what is absurd. Please be assured, I am no fool."

"Of course not, Impewator."

Kane continued, telling the Imperator and the commissioners the events that led to his discovery of the insulating shield and of his theory of how a vital subconscious link between humans had been destroyed. When he had finished, the Imperator stroked his eyebrows thoughtfully before he spoke.

"Even if I accept your evidence, subject to verification, your theory seems far-fetched in the extreme. The alienness of the elements you found in your skulls does not, by itself, implicate the Chirpones, especially if you cannot identify the method by which this irradiation was accomplished."

"Ah, but I can, Imperator. It has been under our noses from the start of the plague. Something the majority of Earthmen have been exposed to not once but many times—something which, for the last ten months, has become the entertainment rage of all Earth. I'll wager that even you have indulged in this novel form."

"The Shul-Rubid tri-d device?" Tulley exploded, and then winced at the loudness of his own voice.

"That's right."

"And I've been using it for training purposes all along," the commissioner groaned.

"Nearly everyone has been exposed in either an entertainment or an educational capacity to the device since the Chirpones first imported it nearly a year ago. Our scientists have studied it and can discover no reason why it should work."

"But, Mr. Kane," the Imperator put in, "my agents routinely inspected the device, along with every other item imported by the Chirpones soon after the trouble started. They found only harmless radiations—analogues of Earth elements, I believe the report said."

"That is true, Imperator. By themselves, the elements are quite harmless. But in combination, and in the presence of some catalyzing agent probably present in the lining of the brain next to the skull, the radiations become deadly. Because no one has suspected an actual neuro-electric network of linkages between humans, your investigators were not looking for something that could disrupt that network. They were looking for something that could directly affect the individual brain and, like everyone else, including the pathologists, they overlooked the wrapping in favor of the package."

Hysrac stepped forward. "Even if the Shul-Wubid device is at fault, I categowically deny any knowledge. We are a simple twading culture—we know nothing of the high technology of the Shul-Wubid . . ."

"You know nothing of the Shul-Rubid because there are no Shul-Rubid. Your ships have traveled no farther than our ships because your ships *are* our ships, in disguise, obtained by secret agreement from the Centaurans and remodeled by your faithful slaves. You never even had ships until that party of Centaurans crash-landed on your planet."

"Well, Impewator, I think we hardly need hear more of this. Mr. Kane has clearly taken leave of his senses."

"If that's so, then you have nothing to fear from my ravings. Nothing to fear, either, from permitting the Imperator to board your ship and see for himself. It was the perfect opportunity, wasn't it—that crash-landing. You had to get off the planet and yet you could not build the ships yourselves. The Krythians were able to build the simple tri-d device for you, but they could never manage anything as large and complex as a spaceship . . ."

"Simple? Weally, Mr. Kane, your own scientists have declared their utter perplexity with how the Shul-Wubid device works, and yet you call it simple?"

"It *is* simple because it was built for only one purpose—to impregnate human skulls with a radiation shield. Our scientists were confused because it *seemed* to do something entirely different."

"Then how do you account for the amazing three-dimensional images which we assumed were cast by the device?" The Imperator asked.

"I was just coming to that . . ."

At that instant the first Tulley broke from his statuelike pose into a run, racing around the top of the chamber for the door, which had remained jammed open after Pendrake's entrance.

"Stop!" thundered the Imperator. When the fake commissioner did not stop, the Imperator signaled and two of his praetorians drew their blasters and fired together. The two beams splashed against the chrome wall behind the running figure, bubbling the metal outward in a shower of molten drops. Then the imposter was gone through the door.

The praetorians whirled in supplication while others from the guard hurried in pursuit.

"Imperator, I could not have missed!"

"Forget it," Kane shouted. "Let him go; you can no more catch him than the police at the Planetary Trade Center could have caught that man whose touch supposedly killed a Chirpone months ago. That was the cleverest ruse of all, Hysrac. What an ingenious way to keep us from approaching you and learning the truth."

"Impewator, I will hear no more of this," the Chirpone screamed. "If you do not stop him, we will turn back the shipment of sewum and leave you all to your destwuction."

The Imperator started to speak and then paused, doubt twisting his face.

Kane swallowed in a dry throat. "You can drop the lisp now, Hysrac. We are no longer fooled by your cute appearance and babyish charm . . ."

"Silence, Kane. I'm inclined to agree with trader Hysrac. Your charges are outrageous. There is much here that does not please me—time wastes while Earth falls and you spin fantastic tales. Your house of cards lacks the most central support—motive. I am well versed in Ambassador Brace's intelligence reports on Archepellan. They give no hint why the Chirpones should wish to destroy Earth, and many reasons why they would not do such a thing—if indeed they could."

"They do not wish to destroy Earth, Imperator—only its people. That was the most baffling point of all. Why should the Chirpones, who already possess a virginal forested planet which they appear to populate only thinly, wish to take over our planet? When I realized the nature of their deception, their reason for attacking us became instantly clear." He turned to Hysrac. "Impersonating Clayton Tulley was a desperate gamble which my investigation forced upon you at the last minute. Now you've lost the gamble and all the pieces are in place."

The Imperator frowned. "You are as murky as a professor, Kane. What is this supposed deception which took in the entire human race, including my best agents, while unveiling itself to you alone?"

"I'll illustrate, Imperator. Otherwise you'll be sure I'm crazy. Hysrac, there is a paper on the table beside you. Pick it up, crumple it into a ball and toss it over here."

"I shall do nothing of the kind. I am not under your authowity to be commanded like a slave."

"Pick it up and I will denounce everything I have said; admit that I am a liar and a traitor."

"I do not see . . ."

"Just crumple it up and throw it over. I have everything to lose and you nothing."

The seconds passed. Kane stared at the Chirpone; Hysrac did not move. After a moment had gone by in silence, Kane turned back to the Imperator. "He has not picked up the paper because he *cannot* pick it up. He cannot pick it up *because he does not really exist!*"

Chapter Nineteen

Decorum in the council chamber broke down. The Imperator recovered first and bellowed the room to silence.

"Explain yourself at once," he commanded Kane.

"Hysrac is a projection, Imperator. An illusion. All Chirpones are projections produced by the same force that provided the tri-d images for the so-called Shul-Rubid device."

"Of all the . . . Projections? How? By whom?"

Kane glanced at Hysrac, who had not moved. "There is another very popular item, besides the tri-d device, which the Chirpones have introduced to our planet. You have all seen the musal trees—no one of any status is without at least one. In fact there are several in the center courtyard below this very council room. Imperator, they are probably in your gardens—tokens of esteem from the Chirpones, no doubt. A musal tree was present on the occasion I mentioned earlier outside the Trade Center, and there were musals in the hold of the vessel on which I traveled to Archepellan. I'll wager that wherever you find a Chirpone or a tri-d device, you'll find a musal tree."

"Are you suggesting that these plants are *intelligent?* That they are engaged in a plot to destroy the human race?"

"Yes, Imperator, I am. It has been thought for some time that our Terran plants may be receptive to emanations from human beings. Why not a powerful alien species of plant who not only is sensitive to these emanations but knows how to disrupt them? In a universe of infinite variety, surely there is a planet where plants bested animals in the evolutionary race to intelligence. Such plants would possess complex structures so alien that we would never guess at their function, especially since we are not prepared to look for intelligence in vegetation. Such plants might well be capable of creating illusions with light and sound waves; projections which could give the appearance of a life form harmless and affable—nonthreatening to the extent of cowardice; illusions which appeared to talk and walk but could never touch the ground, or the chairs they sat in or the doors that were always opened for them by their bodyguards. Archepellan is the planet and the musal trees are its rulers. Sometime, perhaps long ago, the musal overran Archepellan—choked every inch of arable land with their roots. When the colonists from Alpha Centauri landed, the trees had their chance to spread to another planet, to wipe out another competitor by the only means possible—subtlety and illusion. Once Earth became a planet of corpses—a world doomed to perpetual quarantine by a frightened galaxy, the musal would be free to follow their innate urge to reproduce. Our bodies would become their *fertilizer.*"

The chamber was still. Hysrac remained immobile behind his wall of Krythians, whose blasters now covered the entire room. The Imperator shook his head slowly. "And the Krythians . . . ?"

"The only *native* animal life form, besides the nearly extinct thrax, left on Archepellan. They were not paid mercenaries from off-planet, but dull-witted and manually skilled creatures whose minds were open to the control of the spreading musal trees, whose hands became the instruments to open doors for their illusory masters, to wield blasters—also obtained from the Centaurans—to shape primitive buildings from the quarries of Archepellan to fool the human visitors. They are the last remnant of the losers in the evolutionary struggle on Archepellan. If they become too numerous, the musal compel them into the forests where they are eaten by the thrax. A tight balance is maintained. I myself have felt the pull on my mind while I was on the planet, the feeling of peace and lassitude which could have held me on the planet—as it did the Centauran expedition. Fortunately our minds are too advanced for direct control. . . ."

There was an audible gasp in the chamber as Hysrac popped out of existence. "This has gone far enough." The new voice was deep and chilling, edged with subsonics which created a feeling of unease in the pit of the stomach. The voice seemed to come from everywhere in the room. "Mr. Kane, we congratulate you, but your perceptiveness has won an earlier death for everyone in this room. At least you may now understand why you must die. During our sleeps, equaling years of your time, we would dream of spreading our spores on the rich soil of an empty planet and continuing our arrested development. Imagine our shock, when your colonist ship landed, at the concept of a species *both* mobile and intelligent—unlike the witless Krythians whose functions you so accurately described. Some among us had speculated that on a few other worlds animal species might actually have developed intelligence, though I must admit to being among the skeptics. The Krythians had for years tended our needs, assisting as we experimented with hybrid strains, moving our seed where the airborne spores could not, redistributing water during local droughts and performing many other functions beyond the reach of stationary creatures such as ourselves. Thus it was natural for us, during the days following the crash, to study and probe the colonists, to wonder how we might best induce them to serve our needs. We discovered through their talk, the nature of their mother planet, Earth. Our powers over the minds of humans are limited—we moved slowly, inducing in the crash survivors a feeling of peace and gratitude; depending on the Chirpone image we projected, drawn from their minds as an innocuous and even lovable persona. We let the gentle philosophies we articulated through the projections, and our ability to subtly affect emotion, do what the force of our wills could not. Among the refugee colonists were more than enough who could, under innocent pretexts, provide us the ships, the pilots and, to some extent, the technologies we needed for every aspect of our design. The animosity toward Earth we found in the expressions of the colonists aided our efforts considerably, necessitating only gentle nudges where more force would otherwise have been required.

"Now we are on Earth. In only a short time more we will be free to spread our seed—to fill your planet with our species. Unfortunately, the device which Mr. Kane and Dr. Vogelsang have assembled would reverse the process we have so laboriously set in motion, even at this late hour. Therefore, all of you must die."

The Imperator could not find his voice; even the praetorian guard seemed frozen in place. The Krythians aimed their blasters for a sweep of the chamber. As if in a nightmare, Kane struggled against his dead tongue, willing it to cry out as he groped at the comweb in his V-coat.

"Now—NOW!"

A scream echoed through the chamber and died. The Krythians dropped their blasters and fell to all fours, scuttling under tables and crawling to cower like frightened animals against the walls of the chamber. The paralysis fell from everyone at once.

A grinning Tulley gripped Kane's arms; he shouted above the babble. "What did you do?"

Kane felt the strength drain out of him as the megastim reaction finally set in. Tulley had to bend close to hear his answer.

"Beth . . . in the courtyard . . . just blasted the musal trees to ash."

Chapter Twenty

(Epilogue)

It wasn't over. Two weeks after Kane had unmasked the musal conspiracy, Earth continued to tremble in the aftershocks of near calamity. Jails, prisons and the hastily erected camps and stockades were still jammed as the criminal justice system struggled to sort "plague offenders" from real criminals. Hospitals were full of shock and trauma casualties of the human race's hag-ridden war on itself. The effects of destruction and disruption of vital services could not be undone in a moment: phone lines were still down, commerce in food and other goods was resurging only slowly; the merchant districts of most cities were still pocked with burnt-out shops, and would be for some time to come. Most importantly, the staggering job of releasing almost every human on the planet from solitary confinement within his own skull was far from finished. Vogelsang's prototype device had been modified and improved by the engineers, and military planes equipped with powerful wave broadcasters had begun a saturation campaign of low flyovers all over the globe.

Kane sat in the nearly empty level-six dining room of the casino with Beth, Tulley and Pendrake, and considered all of these things, and was depressed. There had been a certain desperate excitement in his quest for the solution to the plague—a monomaniacal high from which he had now crashed into long and dreary aftermaths. He sipped coffee and tried to answer the questions of the others, which there was only now time to ask, and wished that it was all really over.

"What I don't understand," Beth said, "is what made you pull that stunt on Tulley's double—when he first came back to the office after the real Tulley had been knocked out? You know, when you reminded him how you'd saved his life, but you really hadn't. Knowing it wasn't really Tulley is what clued you in to the whole projection business, but why did you decide to test him in the first place if the illusion was so perfect?"

"I owe that one to the compusayer," Kane replied. "While the real Tulley was out and before the ersatz one came back, the compusayer broke into a conversation Pendrake and I were having—said something about riots in the Russian sector, I believe. When it realized Tulley wasn't in the office, it shut itself off again, *except for body ident monitoring.* It said it would key itself to Tulley; when the commissioner returned, the compusayer should have identified him and broken in with its urgent bulletin. When it didn't, I knew something was wrong. At first I thought it was a human imposter, but then I realized that such perfection of voice, features and characteristics could not be the work of another human."

Kane sipped his coffee, suddenly needing its warmth.

"At that point a lot of other things began to make sense, like how a search party of Chirpones—without their ever-present Krythians, mind you—could suddenly appear in the middle of a forest only moments after the thrax failed to kill us. Or how Esryhon could have appeared outside Rathis' room several minutes before Pendrake, who left at the same time. About then I realized I had never seen a Chirpone open a door or perform any other physical manipulation for himself. It also explained the incident in front of the Planetary Trade Center which set up their need for isolation so perfectly. How could the man who somehow broke through tight police lines and actually ran up and touched a Chirpone despite the wall of armed Krythians escape a small army of pursuing cops who were spraying everything with their blasters? That man was never found, despite good camera shots of his face and a hundred witnesses—that bothered me, especially since I got flattened the instant I tried to shake hands with Hysrac. The whole thing was faked, of course. The man was as phony as the Chirpone—and the mush he supposedly turned him into. They were faked by the nearby musal trees—the object of the ceremony. It was a perfect bluff; no one dared suggest, after that terrible incident, that there was anything strange about the Chirpones' wish for isolation." Kane realized he'd been talking without interruption for some time; that the others were listening attentively. Oddly, talking seemed to lift his depressed mood a bit. "In a way," he continued, "we should have guessed earlier that the Chirpones might be illusions. The most obvious clue of all was right in front of us—the tri-d device. From the moment we first saw the device, not knowing it was a 'Trojan horse,' we might have become suspicious at such a technology for producing three-dimensional images. Our mistake was in assuming that the images came from the little olive-drab boxes instead of the musal trees—a natural enough error."

Pendrake took time out from his eating to nod. "What did make you suspicious of the musal trees?"

"In a way, you did. Remember when you picked up that sick geranium on our first trip to New York and went on about how it could sense things? I guess that made an impression that stuck somewhere beneath the surface until the right moment. There were other things, too. The fact that no Chirpone was ever seen very far away from a musal tree . . ."

"But that could have been because the musal were the Chirpones' only food source, just as they claimed," Beth said.

"It was a decent cover story," Kane agreed, "but it wore thin. I found it hard to believe, for example, that the Chirpones had found no way to preserve the fruit, as Hysrac told me on the ship. Carting those potted trees around would have been a major nuisance unless there was some other significance to them. For a while I thought it was because the trees were sacred, but then that didn't seem to mesh with the mechanistic philosophies Hysrac was always spouting."

Kane took another sip of coffee and his eyes strayed to the small section of gaming room that was visible through one of the entrances to the dining room. "Anyway, back to the trees. There were other clues—the complete dominance of the musal over any other plant form, the absence of animals or complex ecological chains, the way my emotions changed when I got into the forest, and another very curious thing. Perhaps you noticed it too, Pendrake."

The alien pursed his lips. "To what are you referring?"

"With a planet full of trees, you'd expect some things to be made of wood. Nothing was. No wooden furniture, doors, not even a toothpick."

"Of course. I should have noticed that."

"Not necessarily. Nothing's harder to see than something that isn't there. That was our main trouble all along in a dozen different ways." Kane cast another glance at the gaming tables.

"You took a big chance in the council room," Tulley said, "when you asked Hysrac to pick up that paper. It would have been simple for the musal to project a piece of paper for him to pick up, while blanking out the real one."

"But if he'd wadded the paper up and tossed it over to me as I requested, I would not have been able to pick up the illusion," Kane pointed out. "He still would have been exposed."

"Oh, yeah. That's right."

"Really," Kane went on, "the musal should have had their Krythians blast me the minute I walked in the door."

"But that would have made them look very suspicious to the Imperator," Beth protested.

"It still would have been better for them than what finally happened. The trouble was, they didn't know how much I knew or how much I might have told others. They kept hoping to outbluff me, right up until it was too late."

"There're two other things I don't understand," Tulley said. "First, if the musal knew or even suspected you were hot on their trail, why would they permit you to visit Archepellan?"

"That made me wonder at first, too. It seemed a very open gesture—not the act of a race with something to hide. But the answer is obvious. We were never supposed to get there alive. Major Anders was supposed to kill us—an idea carefully and subtly put into his head by the Chirpones. Ordinarily they could not have persuaded a human to commit murder. As I understand it, their powers were limited to strengthening certain emotions, such as the fear that nearly froze us all during that crucial moment in the council chamber. Anders already hated the Earthies so much that a little push was all that was necessary. They were even able to implant a posthypnotic heart stoppage to remove their tool from inspection. It would have been an unfortunate but unmysterious assassination by a rabid anti-Terran, which would have left the Chirpones free of suspicion. When Anders failed, they did their best to bend my emotions—at one point I considered giving up the whole investigation, sending for Beth and . . ." He trailed off, as Beth eyed him and the others smiled. "Anyway, they also tried their best to prevent us getting off the planet. We still don't know exactly how they sensed things, aside from their symbiosis with the Krythians. Of course, on Archepellan, surveillance was no problem. On Earth we've found plenty of evidence of their canny sense of strategy—they had one or two musal trees at key points all over the planet. That way they could oversee the operation and be in an excellent position to propagate after humanity was gone."

"Of course, when you found them out, the jig was up," Tulley said. "Thanks to your foresight in putting Beth in the garden. A tree can't very well run away and hide, let alone stand and fight. The deception was everything."

"You had another question," Kane reminded him.

"Right. What put you onto the tri-d device?"

"An educated guess. The device was too mysterious–too impenetrable–even for the work of an alien culture. The only thing our scientists had found were the completely 'harmless' radiations–which they falsely supposed were merely a spin-off from the process that caused the tri-d scenes. The radiations were all the box produced; the images were always provided by nearby musal trees. The devices had been on Earth about as long as the plague, despite the clean bill of health given them by the Imperator's scientists. Also, as I thought back, I realized that my first personal experiences with the plague came right after viewing a tri-d show. Evidently some of the effects wore off since I got no further doses–that's why I felt better later; the shield in my skull had not had enough doses to become impenetrable."

Kane noticed Beth's pensive expression. "What's wrong?"

"I was thinking about Hysrac," she replied. "How sweet he was, and how interesting it was to know him. It's hard to believe he never existed."

"The minds behind the deception must surely share some of the characteristics of their creations,"

Pendrake said gently. "What they attempted to do cannot be forgotten, but from their own perspective, the pressures were very great."

"What will become of them—the musal trees, I mean?"

"The last of them on Earth were shipped back to Archepellan days ago," Tulley said. "The planet is under imperial interdict until we can devise a way to study the culture without danger to ourselves. Perhaps some good may yet come out of our association with them. Meanwhile, we'll be watching for musal saplings here on Earth for some time, just in case some of them got ahead of their grand design and dropped seeds."

"I heard them over the comweb," Beth said wistfully, "when I was hiding in the courtyard waiting for Elias' signal. They'll be lonely, chained forever to that one planet."

"We'll find a way to coexist with them," Kane said. "The first meeting between plant and animal intelligence is too special to put on the shelf for long."

"By the way," Tulley put in, "an imperial council is still trying to decide what to do about the Krythians. Should we leave them on Archepellan, in their old symbiosis with the musal, or should we transplant them somewhere else where they can pursue an independent evolution? It's not an easy question."

Kane nodded, his gaze wandering again to the Gal-Tac room. A well-dressed man was lounging by one of the empty boards, no doubt hoping for a game. Kane thought about the purse of one million credits—of what a royal stake it would make, and his heart began to pound at his eardrums.

"What are you going to do with your new-found

wealth?" Tulley asked, as though sensing his thoughts.

"What? Oh, I'm going into business—Elias Kane, Investigations. I'll only take on the big stuff, off-planet and like that."

"Pretty classy. I may even hire you myself."

"Not at my fees." Kane pushed back from the table. "If you'll excuse me, my friends . . ."

"Yes," Beth cut in. "If you'll excuse *us*, we've got plans for the day."

Kane tried not to look sheepish as they got up together and she twined her fingers into his. *How could he have forgotten*? As they strolled off, leaving Pendrake and Tulley to exchange knowing smiles, Kane deliberately chose a course leading away from the gaming tables. Still, there was a thought which he could not entirely suppress: that the games would be there later, if he needed them.

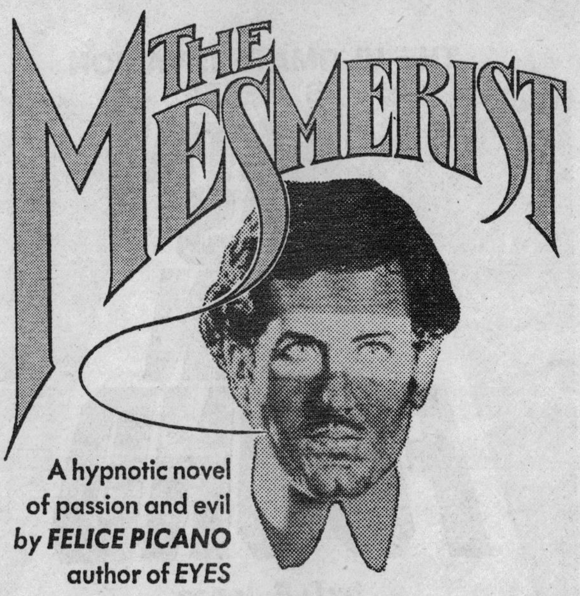
THE MESMERIST
A hypnotic novel
of passion and evil
by FELICE PICANO
author of EYES